CHRISTMAS AT GODDARD DOWNS

A MATURE-AGE CHRISTIAN ROMANCE

JULIETTE DUNCAN

A SUNBURNED LAND SERIES - BOOK 6

FOREWARD

HELLO! Thank you for choosing to read this book - I hope you enjoy it! Please note that as this story is set in Australia, Australian spelling and terminology have been used throughout.

I hope you enjoy the conclusion to the Sunburned Land Series.

Happy reading,
Juliette

BOOKS IN THIS SERIES

Slow Road to Love

Slow Path to Peace

Slow Ride Home

Slow Dance at Dusk

Slow Trek to Triumph

Christmas at Goddard Downs

Beneath the Southern Cross: Dawn of a Sunburned Land Series

Love's Unwavering Hope

Love's Rebellious Spirit

Love's Distant Dream

Love's Precious Moments

Love's Faithful Journey

CHAPTER 1

Kununurra, far north Western Australia

On a steamy December afternoon, Elizabeth Martin parked her red Subaru XV outside the well-maintained weatherboard home where Mary Goddard, the matriarch of the Goddard family, had lived with her daughter and son-in-law for fifteen years.

A fall the week before had damaged the paper-thin skin on the ninety-nine-year-old's left arm and leg. Dr. Thomson had wanted to admit her to the hospital for fear of infection, but stubborn as always, Mrs. Mary, as everyone knew her, insisted she'd be fine.

Elizabeth agreed with the doctor but knew better than to argue with Mary Goddard, who still possessed all her faculties, including her clever mind, sharp tongue, and quick wit.

As Elizabeth opened her car door and climbed out, a wall of intense heat, heavy with the scent of jasmine, engulfed her, but she was used to it, having lived in the far north of Australia most of her life. She grabbed her medical bag and headed towards the white timber gate as Frank Goddard, Mary's eldest son, exited the front door and strolled along the flagstone path.

Although Kununurra was a three-hour drive from Goddard Downs, Frank had started visiting his mother regularly. She was in good health, but last month, she'd lost two of her closest friends, both younger by several years. Frank had officiated at their funerals and seemed to realise his mother could go at any time.

Still, he whistled as he walked. But that was Frank.

"Hey, Liz." He jogged a few steps closer and gave a wave. "Mum said you were coming this afternoon. Good to see you."

"And you. How is she today?" Elizabeth hoisted her bag strap over her shoulder and tightened her ponytail.

"Much the same. Still insisting she'll be fine to come for Christmas. You know how she is." His crystal-blue eyes sparkled in his sun-weathered face.

Yep. Elizabeth knew. She also understood his mother's desire to spend Christmas with her family at Goddard Downs where she and her late husband, William, had lived and worked and raised their four children. The cattle station held many memories for her, and perhaps she sensed it might be her last opportunity to spend Christmas there.

"All being well, I'll bring her out tomorrow." Planning to spend Christmas at Goddard Downs as well, Elizabeth had already offered to take Mrs. Mary. Now she wasn't so sure she wanted to spend Christmas with the Goddard family. She loved them. Of course, she did. They were like family to her.

That was the problem. If she went to Goddard Downs, everyone would expect her and Sean to announce their engagement, but things had cooled between them, leaving her wondering if he'd ever propose. She'd even considered popping the question herself, then begun questioning if they were suited. *And* if she could give up her job to live at the cattle station he co-managed with his cousin Olivia.

Did she want to live at Goddard Downs?

And what about Bree's offer to travel the world with her and nurse wherever they found themselves? Elizabeth never cared to travel, but her spirit felt restless. She needed a change, and the idea appealed.

But could she walk away from Sean?

He annoyed her, but she also loved him.

Or at least, she thought she did.

If only God would make it clear what she should do.

Frank opened the car door and rested his hand on the frame, hot air shimmering from the open door. "Great. If there's any problem, call me. I know what my mother can be like."

"She'll be fine."

"You're a legend, Liz." He slid into the driver's seat, then popped back out. "Oh, I almost forgot. I hope you're hungry. Sarah's been baking."

"I wondered what the smell was. I thought it was the boabs."

His gaze turned to the flowering bottle-shaped trees lining the wide street. "Could be a bit of both. The flowers are glorious this year."

Elizabeth nodded. "They certainly are."

He climbed into the vehicle and started the engine, tipping his wide-brimmed hat before driving off.

Elizabeth let out a breath. Time to attend to Mrs. Mary. She headed along the grevillea-lined stone pathway to the front steps.

Before she climbed them, the door opened, and Sarah, Frank's older sister, stepped onto the verandah. "Hi, Liz. I thought I heard someone chatting with Frank. Come in out of the heat."

"Thanks. Looks like a storm's brewing." Elizabeth gestured to the menacing cloudbank approaching from the east.

Standing aside for Elizabeth to pass, Sarah followed her gaze. "They said it could be a doozy."

Great. Just what they needed. Being the wet season, storms were common, but short-lived. This one looked different. "I hope Frank stays ahead of it."

"I doubt he will, but he'll be fine. My brother's used to driving in these conditions."

Elizabeth could only pray Sarah was right. The roads grew dangerous quickly. How many road accident victims had she helped treat over the years? They were mainly tourists unfamiliar with the roads, but even as skilled and experienced as Frank was, one tourist driving too fast on a slippery road could wipe him out.

Sarah followed her down the hallway. Christmas music played on the radio, and silver tinsel framed the kitchen doorway.

"Would you like a drink and some Christmas nibbles before you start?"

"Sounds lovely. Perhaps afterwards?" Elizabeth needed to attend to Mrs. Mary.

"No problem. Mum's expecting you. Let me know if you need anything. I'm boxing up treats to hand out at the carols tonight."

Elizabeth entered the living room while Sarah continued to the kitchen. A neatly decorated Christmas tree dominated one corner, its twinkling lights splashing colour on the wall.

Frail in an oversized upholstered armchair, Mrs. Mary smiled, crinkling up her wrinkled face.

"How are you doing, Mary?" Elizabeth set her bag on the carpeted floor and began inspecting the bloodstained bandages, which had only been changed the day before.

"I'm fine. I'm not sure why everybody's fussing."

Hmm. Mary's voice had weakened since her fall. Was she putting on a brave face? Hiding how she felt?

Probably.

Elizabeth tsked, wagging a finger at her most stubborn—and vulnerable—patient. "You know why. In this heat, the risk of infection is high."

"It's cool in here."

It *was* a lot cooler inside than out. But still.

"And Sarah keeps a clean house."

Elizabeth shook her head and clucked her tongue as she removed the last bandage. "That's not in dispute."

"Good. So, there's no problem."

And that was that. Elizabeth would never win an argument with Mrs. Mary. Instead, she inspected the wound on her arm. "But we still need to be cautious."

"I've had worse wounds than these in my lifetime."

"I'm sure you have. But you weren't ninety-nine then."

"Ninety-nine..." Mrs. Mary sighed. "I keep forgetting my age. Go ahead and do what you must." She turned her head and stared out the window, golden sunlight gleaming on dust motes floating in the air.

Elizabeth removed the gauze. Phew. The wound wasn't nasty. "It's not looking too bad."

"See. I told you." As Mrs. Mary craned to peek, her eyes twinkled.

"You did. We'll give it some air before we redress it. Now, let me look at your other wounds."

"They'll be the same."

"Perhaps, but I still need to check."

Air puffed from Mrs. Mary's thin lips so fast the gentle lady barely contained a raspberry. Then, as Elizabeth sank to the beige carpet to unwrap a leg bandage, Mrs. Mary's cold fingers grasped her shoulder, stilling her administrations. "Now, tell me what's going on between you and my grandson."

Beneath the weight of that frail hand, Elizabeth's shoulders fell. She removed the dressing on Mrs. Mary's leg. "Not much, I'm afraid."

"That's what I heard. I thought you'd be married by now."

Elizabeth's shoulders fell further. So had she. "He hasn't even proposed."

"Silly boy." Mrs. Mary tutted. "I'll have words with him tomorrow. You'll have a ring on your finger by Christmas, mark my words."

Right. He probably hadn't even bought one.

Mrs. Mary squeezed her shoulder. "He does love you. He's just unsure of himself. That's all."

Little surprise there with the way Sean's father, Stephen, belittled him. Elizabeth winced, thinking of how Stephen responded when his older brother appointed Sean manager at Goddard Downs after stepping down. "Why can't Stephen see Sean's changed? Offer encouragement—*just once.*"

"Both men are stubborn ones—all us Goddards are. That makes it hard admitting we're wrong."

"True that." Elizabeth swallowed hard, but she couldn't force down the ache in her chest. Couldn't Stephen see what that would mean to his son? No longer the reckless drunkard who only thought about the next rodeo, Sean changed when he surrendered his life to the Lord. But his father's refusal to believe the change was permanent left him questioning his ability to stay true to his new-found faith.

"By God's grace, one day Stephen's opinion will change, and he'll say so. But until then, Mrs. Mary, you're right. Sean's battle with insecurity is real." Tipping her face up towards the Goddard matriarch, Elizabeth slid her hand atop Mrs. Mary's, pressing her fingers against her shoulder. "I don't know. I'm not sure he's ready for marriage."

"Nobody's ever ready for marriage, but so long as a couple love each other and put God first and they're committed to working through whatever comes their way, they'll succeed." Mrs. Mary angled her head, fixing watery but alert blue eyes onto Elizabeth's. "The question is, do you love him?"

Good question. One Elizabeth had been asking herself for days. How did she know? She'd never been in love before, but when she and Sean were together, her heart swelled, and the world looked different. Better. Brighter. They sparred, but they also laughed and shared things they never shared with anyone else.

Was that love?

She drew a long breath as she redressed Mrs. Mary's wounds. "I think so."

A faraway look slackened the elderly lady's face, smoothing out her wrinkles as if carrying her back in time. "Love's a strange thing, but if you're unsure, ask yourself how you'd feel if you never saw him again."

A weight pressed on Elizabeth's chest. She couldn't imagine it. "I'd feel lost."

Mrs. Mary faced her. "I think you have your answer."

Maybe. But if he wasn't ready, she couldn't force Sean to marry her, could she? Perhaps she *should* go travelling with Bree. Give him space to figure out what he wanted.

But what if he decided it wasn't her?

Could she risk it?

She secured the last bandage and pushed to her feet. "There you go. All done."

"Thank you, dear. Now, Sarah's got some Christmas treats ready for us before you go."

Elizabeth smiled and bent to hug the elderly woman's bony shoulders. "I'll let her know we're ready."

Sarah bustled into the room carrying a tray loaded with Christmas goodies and a pot of tea. She placed the tray on the polished timber coffee table, poured three cups of tea, and insisted Elizabeth fill her plate with the home-baked treats.

"You must think I never eat." Elizabeth laughed as she bit into the Christmas cake, groaning with pleasure when the rich flavours burst in her mouth.

Sarah eased into an armchair and sipped her tea. "I know how hard you nurses work and how little time you have for baking."

That *was* true. When Elizabeth arrived home after a twelve-hour shift, the last thing she felt like doing was cooking. Plus, baking wasn't her forte.

After a pleasant hour, she took her leave and said she'd collect Mrs. Mary the following day to drive her to Goddard Downs for Christmas.

She didn't have the heart to tell her she might not stay.

CHAPTER 2

ith Christmas just two days away, Goddard Downs was bustling. All the family were coming, and Maggie couldn't be more excited. Of course, many still lived and worked on the cattle station, but in the two years since Frank's heart attack, some had moved away. Now, because of the distances involved, months or even years could pass between visits.

Janella, Frank's deceased son's wife, had settled in Darwin, and her restaurant—Julian's Dream, named for her late husband, of course—had become so successful she hadn't been back to the station for over a year. This Christmas, she was leaving Jonah, her protégé, in charge and coming home for two weeks.

And Wade was coming with her.

Maggie and Frank had prayed Janella would find love again after losing Julian in that horrific accident, and Wade seemed like a nice man, although they didn't know him well. Sasha and

Caleb liked him. A good sign since teenagers could be overly protective of their surviving parent.

Visiting Goddard Downs, where Janella and Julian had met as children, married, and raised their family, could be confronting for Wade, but it could also cement his and Janella's relationship. Time would tell.

Running Indigo Downs kept Frank's younger son, Joshua, and his new wife, Stella, busy, but with the imminent arrival of their first child, they'd become even busier in the months ahead.

With Frank no longer managing Goddard Downs, he and Maggie often took a few days and made pastoral visits on their way to and from visiting Joshua and Stella. The vastness of the Kimberley region meant each cattle station was at least several hours' drive from any other, and she and Frank were always welcomed with open arms, although not all the station owners were believers. It didn't matter. Frank had a way of getting alongside people and engaging them in conversation. Many times, they were invited to stay over and formed long-lasting relationships. Who knew how God might use that?

After relinquishing the management of Goddard Downs to Olivia, his one and only daughter, and to Sean, his nephew, Frank had embraced his role as pastor, although Maggie did worry he wasn't getting enough rest. The doctor had advised him to slow down, but that was akin to expecting her three-year-old grandson to sit inside and read a book instead of running around outside with his cousins. What three-year-old boy would choose to do that? Frank was the same. She had to trust God to look after him as he spent his energy looking after others.

And then there was Sean. He'd also embraced his new position after a lifetime of self-doubt. Almost unrecognisable in both appearance and manner, he'd smartened up and took pride in his appearance, although Elizabeth might have had something to do with that. Until recently, she'd been a regular visitor to the station, heading out on her days off from the hospital in Kununurra where she nursed. Everyone had been waiting for an engagement announcement and had almost given up hope. And perhaps they were right. Elizabeth hadn't visited for weeks.

With the way Elizabeth spoke her mind, she and Sean often got into verbal sparring, but never anything serious, and they always ended up in each other's arms. God willing, they'd resolve whatever the problem was because they *did* love each other. Sean had avoided the issue, but he hadn't reverted to handling things with alcohol and anger. He was growing in his understanding of what it meant to be a Christian, and Frank was making a great mentor. But a lifetime of self-doubt and put-downs by his father took time to shrug off.

Maggie smiled as the Land Cruiser pulled up outside the cottage. Although they'd been married for years now, her heart still beat faster when Frank returned after being away. He'd stayed overnight with his sister and brother-in-law in Kununurra. He'd wanted Maggie to go with him, but with Christmas so close and Jeremy and Emma and the children already arrived from Darwin, she couldn't.

She finished tying a pretty bow on the gift she was wrapping for Sasha, a gorgeous calligraphy set she hoped the teenager would appreciate, and hurried outside onto the verandah. Frank had just climbed out, and when he looked up, her heart warmed. How blessed they were to have found each other. She'd never thought she'd love a man again after her thirty-three-year marriage ended in divorce after Cliff's affair with a much younger woman. Frank had also not expected to find love again after losing his Esther when she tried to save Caleb and Sasha from floodwaters when they were younger. But God had blessed them beyond their dreams.

He grabbed his overnight bag from the back seat and loped up the stairs. At the top, he set his bag down and pulled Maggie close, brushing his lips against hers. "Sorry I'm late, darling. I stopped on the way to check the water levels."

She gazed into his crystal-blue eyes. "It's okay. With all these storms circling, I'm glad you made it home safely."

He rubbed her forearms. "You worry too much. It *is* the rainy season."

"Thank goodness we have the bridge, or no one would be coming or going."

"I don't know why I ever doubted it was a good idea."

She chuckled. "Because you don't embrace change, but I'm proud of you. Anyway, come inside." She stepped out of Frank's arms and headed inside. "How's your mum?"

He followed. "As feisty as ever and determined to come for Christmas."

"Did you think she'd change her mind?"

"No, especially as she believes this will be her last."

"I don't know why she thinks that. Her heart's as strong as a mallee bull's." Maggie braced a hand on the marble kitchen counter. "Like a cup of tea before dinner?"

"Do we have time?"

"Dinner's in fifteen minutes, so no."

"And we'd best not be late."

Her chest warmed. "Best not. Olivia won't be happy if we are."

He rolled his eyes. "Some things never change. That daughter of mine got her grit from my mother. I'll freshen up, and we can head over."

Ten minutes later, with him in fresh clothes, his hair slicked back, and smelling of shampoo and cologne, they headed outside. A recent storm had left the ground damp and muddy, and Maggie had to watch where she stepped. "Do you think we could build that carport sometime soon?"

"Are you getting soft in your old age, my love?" His eyes twinkled as he held the passenger door open and helped her climb in.

She almost needed a ladder since she was short and the Land Cruiser was extra high. She'd gotten used to hoisting herself up, but she never turned down his offer of help. After sliding into her seat, she tipped her muddy shoes into view. Yuck, and she'd tried so hard to avoid it. Getting soft had nothing to do with it. Maybe she'd build that carport herself. "We've only been talking about it since we got married. I guess there's no hurry."

He lifted his hand to her cheek. "A bit of mud never hurt anybody."

Said the guy who didn't flinch at helping her clean the floors. She pressed her cheek against his still-callused palm. Wasn't like she could fault his efforts. Still... "Sometimes I daydream about having a nice suburban home with a concrete driveway and a garage."

"You'd give up all of this for that?"

Not a chance. "Never. But I wouldn't complain if you did something about the mud one day."

He caressed her cheek. "Maybe next year."

"That's what you said last year." Frogs croaking in the nearby pond drowned out her words as he closed the door and jumped onto the driver's seat.

While starting the engine, he faced her, his brow creased. "Did I really say that?"

Did he really not remember? She arched a brow. "And the year before."

"I'm sorry. You must think I don't care."

She'd never think that. "Other things take priority."

"How about we get the boys to build it?"

"They're too busy." She waved a hand, batting away her momentary annoyance. "It doesn't matter. As you said, a bit of mud never hurt anybody."

He reached over and squeezed her hand. "I'll see what we can do about it."

She smiled, but she wouldn't hold her breath. Since moving to Goddard Downs, she'd learned to love this harsh but beautiful countryside, and Frank was right. A bit of mud never hurt anybody.

With the homestead an easy ten-minute stroll from their cottage, they'd have walked, but since they never knew when a storm might hit, driving was safer this season. Plus, there was the mud.

He pulled up behind Jeremy and Emma's Land Cruiser. Maggie's son and daughter-in-law and their two children, Sebastian and Chloe, had arrived from Darwin yesterday and were staying in the newest cabin down near the gorge.

Frank jumped down, rounded the vehicle, and opened the door for her, spoiling her as usual. He bent with a flourish. "We might not have a carport, but I can carry you across the mud."

Strong arms swept her up and carried her to the gravel path where he stole a kiss before setting her down.

She wobbled, her cheeks heating while she found her balance. "What will the kids think?"

"Does it matter?" He draped an arm around her shoulders and shepherded her towards the steps.

Breathing in his woodsy scent, she leaned into him. It didn't matter. The family had embraced her in a way she'd not thought possible, and she felt like she belonged. Amazing, given their love for Esther.

Children's laughter and cheerful Christmas music drifted down the hallway along with the aroma of roast beef. With Janella no longer cooking for the family and everyone else busy, they'd employed a full-time chef who also cooked meals for the workers. Patty wasn't as adventurous with her cooking as Janella, but the meals were always tasty and wholesome. But while Patty was on leave, Olivia had taken over the role.

They reached the family room where seven-year-old Isobel launched herself at Frank.

He swung her into his arms and kissed her. "How's my girl?"

"Good. But James is really annoying. He follows me everywhere."

"That's what babies do, darling. He thinks you're amazing and just wants to be with you."

"But he can't play."

"Not yet. Give him time."

She blew out a breath. "I guess I have to be patient. That's what Mummy tells me."

"And she's right, of course."

Maggie grinned. Olivia was always right.

"And what about William? He can play."

"But he's a boy, and he just wants to play with trucks."

"And what do you want to play with?"

"Animals. Mummy said I might get my own chickens for Christmas."

"Did she?"

Isobel nodded. "I heard her talking to Daddy."

"Oh." Frank's brow lifted. "You'll just have to wait and see."

"I hope they'll behave under the tree." The little girl's gaze swung to the Christmas tree in the corner of the room. It nudged the ceiling, and ornaments weighed down almost every branch. Maggie had enjoyed listening to the stories behind them as she'd helped decorate the tree with her daughter Serena, Olivia, and the children. They'd added to the collection, further cementing her and Serena's place in the family.

"I'm sure they'll figure it out." Frank winked at his granddaughter before catching Maggie's gaze.

His special relationship with Isobel always warmed Maggie's heart.

He set the little girl down as Olivia entered the room. Her features had softened since Maggie met her when visiting Goddard Downs to interview her and Janella for the *Country Life Women's Magazine*. Frank's one and only daughter always carried herself with poise, but with three young children, she seemed to have lost some of her stiffness.

Although she still ruled the roost.

"Dinner's ready, everyone. Let's eat while it's hot."

Frank placed his hand on Maggie's shoulder, and they stepped aside while the children heeded Olivia's instructions and raced each other to the dining room.

"The family's growing," Maggie said as they followed.

"It sure is."

And not everyone was there yet. Joshua and Stella were arriving tomorrow morning, as were Janella and Wade with Caleb and Sasha. Mrs. Mary and Elizabeth would be coming in the afternoon.

Frank headed for his spot at the head of the table and, ever the gentleman, held out Maggie's chair for her before taking his own.

They'd extended the polished timber table to fit everyone. Emma and Jeremy sat beside Maggie, and Serena and David sat opposite them beside Olivia, Nate, and Sean. The older children sat at the far end, while the younger children sat with their parents. When the others arrived tomorrow, weather permitting, they'd eat outside. But for now, this was nice.

Frank beamed at those around the table, then held out his hands. "Isn't this lovely? Shall we give thanks?"

Maggie slipped one hand into his and her other into Emma's before bowing her head.

A hush fell around the table as Frank cleared his throat and prayed in a clear, strong voice. "Lord God, we give You thanks for bringing us all together. We thank You for our family, for those who are present, and for those who are yet to arrive. Give them travelling mercies, we pray. Keep them safe on the wet roads. And, Lord, we thank You for the many blessings

You've bestowed on us over the years. We're grateful for them all, and we're grateful for this meal before us. Bless it to our bodies, we pray in Jesus' precious name. Amen."

A round of amens resounded before Olivia stood and announced that everyone should help themselves to the roast meat and vegetables on the platters spread along the table. Retaking her seat, she slid a platter in front of Frank. "You go first, Dad."

He nudged it back to her. "Ladies before gentlemen."

Her blue eyes met his as she held his gaze. "Age before beauty."

"Are you saying I'm old?"

Her brow lifted, but then a grin spread across her face. "Maybe."

"Well, I never." With feigned offence, he retrieved the platter and piled his plate high with Goddard Downs beef and fresh vegetables harvested from Maggie's garden.

Chatter and laughter drowned out the Christmas music, and after the meal, they adjourned to the living room to play games and sing Christmas carols.

Isobel pleaded with Frank to tell them the Christmas story, which he did while the kids sat around him on the floor.

Seated on the faded green leather sofa beside Serena, Maggie sipped her warm tea. He doted on his grandkids, and they adored him. Terrible how close they'd come to losing him while on their extended trip around Australia in their camper years before. The desire to continue that trip had dimmed for them both. Perhaps one day they'd pick up where they left off, but in the meantime, life couldn't be better. God had given Frank new purpose and contented her by surrounding her with family, a good garden, and blessed time with her grand-children, and she also wrote articles for the *Christian Women's Magazine*. Life was good, but she'd not take any day for granted.

Serena leaned closer, flicking hair off her face, revealing the scar on her cheek. "Look at Oliver. Do you think he could get any closer to Frank?"

Maggie's chest swelled as her grandson crowded in beside Frank, sitting cross-legged on the flecked-brown living room carpet. "I doubt it. But he'll need to work hard to keep his place with more little ones coming."

Her head tipping to one side, Serena crinkled up her nose and surveyed the gathering. "Who else is expecting?"

Maggie raised her brow. "You?"

"Mum!" The word rushed out in a whispered gasp as Serena's eyes widened. "How did you know?"

So it *was* true. Maggie resisted the urge to shout *hallelujah*. "I can just tell. I'm right, aren't I?"

Nodding, Serena twined their hands. "But we weren't announcing it yet."

Maggie squeezed her hand. "I can keep a secret. I'm so excited for you, sweetheart." Serena's journey to motherhood had been a circuitous one. She'd followed in Maggie's footsteps and became a journalist. While covering a major story in Paris, she'd been caught in a bomb blast that resulted in third-degree burns to much of her body. Years later, her face was still scarred, although she'd come to terms with it as she underwent a heart transformation, surrendered her life to God, and married her longtime partner, David, who now also shared her faith. After never wanting children, Serena's heart had softened further when little Oliver appeared on the scene. She'd never mentioned having a second child, but Maggie had hoped one would come along.

Serena slipped her arm through Maggie's. "David's over the moon."

"I bet he is. Talking of your husband, where is he?"

"Outside, chatting with Sean."

Sean. A sigh escaped despite the moment's joy. "Do you know what's going on with him? He's seemed out of sorts of late."

"Not really, but I think he and Liz are having problems."

Maggie's shoulders fell. "I didn't want to believe the rumours. Let's pray they can figure it out. I'd hate to see them break up."

"So would I. There's even talk of Elizabeth going overseas."

Maggie's shoulders dropped further. "Does Sean know?"

Serena shrugged. "I'm not sure."

"I'd so hoped we'd be celebrating their engagement this Christmas."

"We all were. But miracles do happen, and it *is* Christmas."

True, but… "We might need to help God along a little."

"Mum!" Serena jostled her. "You can't do that!"

"I know." Maggie scrunched up her nose. "But it doesn't stop me hoping for a good outcome."

Serena nudged her in the ribs. "Just don't meddle."

"Who said anything about meddling?"

"Mum!"

"Okay." Maggie huffed at Serena's raised voice and rolled her eyes as Frank eyed them. "I promise."

Maggie sipped her tea while Frank, who'd just finished his

story, pretended to have trouble getting to his feet. All the children were helping him before they fell in one big heap.

Serena straightened. "Oh no. Oliver's underneath."

Maggie held her back. "He'll be fine."

And he was. His cheeky face emerged moments later. "Mum! Look at me! I'm underneath Grandpa."

"I can see that. I hope you're not squashed."

"I'm not." He ducked under Frank's legs and disappeared, emerging on Frank's other side, a Christmas ornament from the tree dangling from his ear. "Look at me. I'm a Christmas tree."

"It's time for bed, little tree." With a shake of her head, Serena pushed to her feet and reached for him, but he darted under the tree before she could grab him. "Three-year-olds!"

"It's Christmas. Don't be too hard on him." Frank motioned to Oliver to come out, and without any further fuss, he did.

"I wish I had Frank's way with kids."

Maggie faced her. "You do. Don't underestimate the gift God's given you." After much soul-searching, tears, and torment, Serena discovered the new path God set before her. She now headed up a training program for Indigenous youth, and the kids loved her.

"But it's different with your own." Picking Oliver up, she hugged and kissed him as he clung to her.

"Maybe. Oh, here's David." Maggie peered behind her darkhaired son-in-law for Sean, her heart falling when he didn't follow.

She didn't miss the look David and Serena shared. They knew more about what was going on than Serena had told her.

On their way home, Maggie asked Frank what he knew.

He shook his head. "I thought everything was hunky-dory."

"Hmm. I'm not so sure. We'd better say an extra prayer for Sean and Elizabeth tonight."

Frank reached over and squeezed her hand. "We can absolutely do that."

CHAPTER 3

That night, Sean tossed and turned. When one a.m. rolled around and he was still awake, he climbed out of bed and sat on his porch. Like a rippled ribbon of light, beams from the half-moon shone through the trees, making silhouettes of them. His mind elsewhere, he stared at the silhouettes unseeing.

Why was it so hard to propose to Elizabeth? He loved her, and she loved him. When they were together, he felt energised, so what was holding him back?

Self-doubt.

It had plagued him his entire life, and although Uncle Frank believed in him and God loved him, some things were hard to shrug off. Like his father's words... "You'll never amount to anything, boy."

He should chuck it all in and go back on the circuit where he belonged. Whatever made him think he could manage Goddard Downs? Sure, everyone said he was doing a great job, but what did he really know about managing a multimillion-dollar enterprise? He'd fooled everyone into believing he knew what he was doing. But he was a fraud, and they'd find out.

He couldn't expect Elizabeth to marry him. She deserved better.

David's words came back to him. "Don't let fear steal your happiness."

Was that what it was? Fear? Fear of what? Failure? Of letting her down? How many times had she told him she believed in him? Loved him.

David had asked who he was listening to.

Who *was* he listening to?

Many people over the years had influenced him, some good, some not so good. Like his father. And now voices in his head told him he was a fraud.

David told him to ignore them, to listen instead to what God said about him. God believed in him and loved him so much that, if Sean had been the only person alive, God still would've sent Jesus to die for him.

Why would He do that?

He wasn't worth it.

Eyes flashed in the bushes, but he didn't flinch. Animals didn't scare him. Not even ones with teeth. Or the crazy ones he used to ride.

Could he leave all of this and return to the circuit? Last time he'd ridden, he'd broken his arm.

And now he was older.

Everyone would think him stupid.

Maybe he *was* stupid.

Maybe his father was right.

Eyes flashed again, this time closer.

He stood and fisted his hand. "Come on. I'm not scared." His voice, loud in the still of the night, scared the animal away.

Was he any different to the creature? One harsh word, and he'd flee?

No. He was the same.

MORNING CAME. He dragged himself out of bed. As he dressed in his work gear, he paused by the photo of him and Elizabeth at Purnululu National Park. He picked it up from the dresser. Man, she was gorgeous.

She deserved so much better than him. He set the photo down. Turned it over.

He'd tell her it was over. Not a great thing to do at Christmas, but he couldn't leave her dangling.

And he'd resign and return to the circuit.

He skipped breakfast and headed out. The cattle had been moved to higher ground to avoid the risk of footrot during the wet season. The rivers and creeks were bursting, so the livestock had to remain in a safe area. Easier said than done when they were scattered over such a vast area. Often, he and David would take the chopper to check on them, but the chopper was in for repairs, so that left the quad bikes. Or horses. With the ground still sodden after last night's storm, horses were the safer option.

After closing the door, he headed down the steps and strode to the stables.

David was already there, and both horses were saddled. He tossed Sean a set of reins. "Thought I'd get a head start."

"Thanks, mate. I had a rough night."

"I can tell." David's brow lifted as he mounted his horse.

"Great." Sean rolled his eyes. He geed the horse, and they set off up the track, stopping only when they reached the fence line.

He glanced both ways. "Looks good, but we'd best check the gully. I don't trust this mob."

"I don't either. We don't need any more escapees. Especially not over Christmas."

"Come on." He pointed the horse along the fence line. "We don't have time to waste."

David caught up and rode alongside. "What's the hurry?"

There wasn't any. Most of the jobs had been done in the lead-up to Christmas so they could relax, but restlessness spurred him on. "I'm going back on the circuit. I'm going to end it with Liz."

"You don't mean that. You're not thinking clearly."

"She deserves better than me."

"You're listening to those voices again. Did you pray about it like I said?"

"I tried, but God didn't listen."

"How do you know?"

"Dunno." With his jaw set, Sean geed his horse and sped away.

CHAPTER 4

*S*ometime during the night, Elizabeth made her decision. She'd take Bree up on her offer. She'd leave Kununurra and Sean and go travelling. He didn't love her, otherwise he would have proposed by now. She couldn't—she *wouldn't*—hang around waiting when he might never pop the question.

But as she woke to a kookaburra's laugh, deep sadness gnawed her insides. From the moment she'd met Sean, she'd been drawn to the dark-haired diamond in the rough. She never wanted him to lose his raw ruggedness, but she'd loved witnessing the transformation in his life. He was a cowboy at heart. He took risks. So why wouldn't he take a risk on her?

Lord, what am I to do?

Pushing back the bedcovers, she wriggled up and leaned against her pillows, grabbed her Bible, and opened it. If only God would speak to her, but that was unlikely. But maybe she'd find an answer in Scripture. The Bible fell open at James chapter 1, a book she knew well as her weekly Bible study group recently studied it. Her gaze went to verses five to eight:

If any of you lacks wisdom, you should ask God, who gives generously to all without finding fault, and it will be given to you. But when you ask, you must believe and not doubt, because the one who doubts is like a wave of the sea, blown and tossed by the wind. That person should not expect to receive anything from the Lord. Such a person is double-minded and unstable in all they do.

Yep. That was her. She'd asked, but she must be doubting because that's how she felt. Tossed about like a wave. Flip-flopping. One minute, never wanting to leave Sean—the next, deciding to travel overseas.

She bowed her head. *Lord, I don't want to be like this. I need clarity. Guidance. Wisdom. But I also can't make Sean love me. If he doesn't want to spend his life with me, please show me what I'm to do, because I do love him. And that's the truth. It'd kill me to leave him, but I can't be near him if we're not together. I'm so confused. Give me peace and help me know what to do. In Jesus' precious name. Amen.*

After a shower and a breakfast of Vegemite toast and juice, she dressed in her uniform and headed out. She was doing a half-shift this morning before collecting Mrs. Mary and driving to Goddard Downs. She'd already packed and carried her bags to her car and loaded them, including the one containing her Christmas gifts for the family, into the boot.

Rostered to work in the children's ward, she needed to be bright and bubbly, so she put her relationship woes aside as she pulled into the hospital carpark. A busy shift would help her forget him for a few hours.

Her heart went out to the children spending Christmas in

the hospital. Those well enough to be discharged had already left, but twelve remained, including little Lucy, who'd broken her back falling off a climbing frame, and Brock, who'd been hit by a car two days ago and remained in a critical condition.

After bidding her fellow staff members a happy Christmas at the end of her shift, she headed to Sarah's house to collect Mrs. Mary. She was sitting on the front verandah when Elizabeth pulled into the driveway. The gate was open, so she drove in and stopped beside the house.

No going back now. Climbing out, she smiled and put on a happy voice. "You look brighter today."

Mrs. Mary beamed. "I *feel* brighter. Maybe it has something to do with it being Christmas."

"Maybe." But perhaps it was that Mrs. Mary's wounds were healing. No blood had oozed through the bandages. "We can leave your dressings and do them when we get to Goddard Downs."

"Sounds good to me. I'm packed and ready to go. Sarah and Mick are ready to leave as well." They were spending Christmas with his family in Katherine, a five-hour drive east.

"I'll grab your bag if you like. Save you getting up."

"Thank you, dear. You're a gem."

If only Sean thought that.

"I'll just be a jiffy." Elizabeth opened the door and almost ran headlong into Sarah, who'd appeared from the front room carrying an overnight bag. "Whoops. I didn't see you. Sorry."

"No problem. I heard you, so thought I'd bring Mum's bag out." She leaned in closer. "She's been sitting out there waiting for the past two hours."

Elizabeth frowned. "I'm not late, am I?"

"No." Sarah waved her free hand, also shooing Elizabeth away when she reached for the bag. "She's just eager."

"Right. Best not keep her waiting, then."

"I hope she doesn't cause any problems."

"She'll be fine." Elizabeth turned to head back out. "At least she has a nurse with her."

"Thank goodness for that. I wouldn't be comfortable with her going if you weren't there for her."

Elizabeth just smiled. How could she leave early now? She'd have to stay for the full three days, whether she and Sean were talking or not. Wonderful. Perhaps Mrs. Mary might want to come back early. Unlikely, but possible.

She helped Mrs. Mary to her feet and down the ramp along the front of the house. Sarah and Mick had put it in soon after Mrs. Mary came to live with them, even though she insisted she could manage the steps.

Elizabeth and Mrs. Mary walked at a snail's pace. Having already placed her mother's bag on the back seat, Sarah now helped settle her into the front passenger seat.

"There you go. Have a great time, and merry Christmas." She kissed her mother on the cheek before straightening.

Mrs. Mary squeezed her hand. "And you, luv. I'm sorry we're not spending it together."

"You'll have a wonderful time with Frank and the family. Just take care of yourself."

"Pshaw." Mrs. Mary waved. "I will. Don't worry about me."

"I'll try not to." Sarah stood back as Elizabeth climbed into the driver's seat and started the car, waving as she drove off.

Before turning from the driveway, Elizabeth faced her companion. "So, what would you like to listen to?"

"Whatever you want, dear. But how about some Christmas music?"

"Sure." Elizabeth had a playlist ready and selected it. Old Christmas carols she hoped Mrs. Mary would like, as she doubted she'd go for the modern jazzed-up ones.

By the third song, Mrs. Mary harrumphed. "Is your plan to put me to sleep?"

"No."

"Well, put on some of those new songs. These would make a baby nod off."

"Sorry." Elizabeth's lips twitched up. "I thought you'd like them." But how wrong could she be.

Arms folded across her chest, Mrs. Mary jutted up her chin. "You thought wrong."

Driving across the bridge spanning the Ord River, dam sparkling on her left, river weaving into the distance on her right, Elizabeth laughed and shook her head. "No problem."

When she selected her other playlist, Mrs. Mary grinned and started bopping. "That's better. I'm not in my grave yet, you know."

"Oh, I know."

"So, how was your morning?"

Elizabeth slowed as the car in front turned into the road leading to the riverside park. Then she told her about the sick children and how sad it was they'd be spending Christmas in the hospital.

"At least they have a hospital. When my kids were little, we had to call the Flying Doctor if they were sick."

"And did you?"

"Once. When Frank was three, he had a fever that wouldn't break. We thought he'd die."

Having recently treated a child with a high fever, Elizabeth could imagine how they felt. "Meningitis?"

Mrs. Mary hugged her arms tighter around herself, her thin lips wobbling as she nodded. "He survived, but we were worried about him."

"God had things planned for him to do."

Mrs. Mary nodded. "I'm so proud of him. I never thought he'd give up managing the station, but he's taken to pastoring so well it's hard to imagine he ever did anything else."

"All that life experience is being put to good use."

"He *has* been through a lot. But let's stop talking about him. What about *you*? Have you come to any conclusions?"

"About Sean?"

"Yes. About that grandson of mine."

Where did she start? "Not really. I thought I had, but then I wasn't sure. I need to talk with him because it's up to him where we go from here."

"I'll be praying for you." Mrs. Mary rummaged in her purse for a handkerchief and dabbed at the sweat on her forehead. "And I'll have words with him myself."

Elizabeth didn't dare turn the air-conditioning up any higher, or Mrs. Mary would start shivering. She twisted her grip on the steering wheel, unsure how well such a talk would go down. She let out a low breath and loosened her clenched hands. After all, Mrs. Mary *did* have a good relationship with Sean. Just like Elizabeth had had with her own grandmother before she died.

With Elizabeth's father dead and her mother remarried and

living overseas, the elderly woman had become like her own grandmother of late. Having someone as old and wise as Mrs. Mary as her mentor was comforting.

Menacing clouds loomed in the rear-view mirror. Elizabeth had hoped they'd stay ahead of today's storm, but it didn't seem likely. Mrs. Mary's chin dropped to her chest, and soft snores sounded as the sealed road gave way to gravel, soon to be slippery and muddy if that storm caught them.

Elizabeth glanced in the mirror again and slowed. She had precious cargo on board, and she'd never forgive herself if something happened to Mrs. Mary. At least she had a new car. Sean had long wanted her to upgrade her old one, and she'd relented.

The storm overtook them, and she slowed further and turned the wipers to full speed. Mrs. Mary woke as rain pelted the windscreen.

"I must have nodded off. Are you okay, dear?"

"I'm fine. The storm should pass quickly."

"Let's hope so." Mrs. Mary tipped her head to the sunroof. A chortle burst from her chest, and she clapped as lightning flashed. "It's a beauty, though, isn't it?"

Elizabeth's lips twitched up. She didn't dare glance at her companion, not when the sloshy road required her full attention, but she *could* hope Mrs. Mary's zeal for all life threw at her was contagious.

By the time they reached the turn-off to Goddard Downs, the rain had stopped and the sky had cleared, but the road remained slippery and muddy. Thank goodness for the expensive tyres the salesman had talked her into.

Twenty minutes later, she pulled up in front of the homestead, parking as close to the steps as possible to reduce the muddy trek. The car parking area was gravel, but a red, muddy sludge covered it.

Perhaps one of the men—maybe even Sean—might carry Mrs. Mary up the steps?

At the thought of him, Elizabeth's heart skipped a beat. Concentrating on the road had kept her from thinking about him, but now with the prospect of seeing him, her pulse raced.

That was a good sign, wasn't it? It showed she had strong feelings for him despite her annoyance.

She opened her door and climbed out, stretched, and then looked expectantly up at the verandah. Instead of Sean, her heavily pregnant cousin appeared. "Hey, Stell. Can you get someone to help me with Mrs. Mary?"

"Sure. I'll grab Olivia."

Elizabeth frowned. Where were all the men? Not that Olivia wasn't strong. Living and working on a cattle station made the women almost as strong as the men, and besides, Mrs. Mary was a featherweight. But it was… odd.

Moments later, Olivia hurried down the steps and hugged Elizabeth. "How was the drive?"

"Not too bad."

"Glad you made it safely. That storm was a doozy."

Elizabeth nodded. It sure was.

Olivia opened the passenger door and beamed at her grandmother. "Good to see you, Gran. How are you doing?"

"Fit as a mallee bull. I can get myself out."

"I'm not so sure about that." Olivia jammed her hands on her hips. "Liz? What do you think?"

"I'd like to see you stop her. She's as independent as they come."

Olivia chuckled. "And don't we know it."

Mrs. Mary did her best, but the two women helped her up the steps. Against Olivia's five foot ten, Mrs. Mary seemed even tinier. And frailer. By the time she reached the top, she was breathless.

"You should take a break, Gran." With a hand braced under Mrs. Mary's elbow, Olivia furrowed her brow.

"I'm fine. Just give me a moment."

Olivia leaned closer to Elizabeth and lowered her voice. "Did she bring her walker?"

"It's in the boot. I'll grab it."

"Thanks. We don't need another situation today."

"Situation?" Elizabeth stopped in her tracks. "Why? What's happened?"

Her shoulders inching up, Olivia palmed a hand over her face. "Sean's missing."

CHAPTER 5

*W*ait. What had she said? *Missing?* Her chest tightening, Elizabeth gasped. "What do you mean?"

Olivia let out a heavy breath. "Come inside, and I'll tell you."

Mrs. Mary grabbed Elizabeth's wrist. "I know my grandson. He'll be okay wherever he is."

Was this his way of telling her it was over between them? What a coward. And what a way to ruin Christmas. Roiled heat coursed through her. But she was making judgments without knowing the facts. That wasn't like her. Still… *how* could he be missing?

She rubbed her other hand behind her neck. "Let's hope so. Now, come on. Let's get you inside. I'll grab your walker."

"Don't worry about it. I've got my stick."

"Okay, but we'll walk with you."

"You worry too much. Both of you."

"We don't want you to have another fall, Gran." Olivia paced beside her down the hallway.

Elizabeth followed. Despite all the Christmas decorations, Christmas songs, and Christmas baking scents, a heavy lump had settled in her stomach.

What if she never saw him again?

No. She couldn't think like that. Of course, he was all right. Wherever he was. There'd be some reasonable explanation. There had to be. *Lord, please look after Sean. You know where he is and what's going on with him.*

After a visit to the bathroom, they headed to the lounge room and were settling Mrs. Mary into an armchair when Olivia's phone rang.

Could it be news of Sean? Elizabeth's heart pounded as she tried not to think the worst.

Olivia stepped away and spoke as Elizabeth attended to Mrs. Mary while keeping an eye on Olivia. "I'll get you a cup of tea, and then I'll redress your wounds."

"Don't worry about me. I can see your mind's on other things."

Was it that obvious? Even the sunny-yellow walls and soothing spring-green curtains couldn't brighten her downcast mood. "Right, but I do need to redress them. The last thing we want is for an infection to take hold."

"You win." Mrs. Mary raised a finger. "But don't fuss. Besides, plenty of others here can look after me. Not that I need looking after, mind you."

Elizabeth bent and hugged Mrs. Mary's frail shoulders, Mrs. Mary who found joy in a dangerous storm and smiled through her pain. No wonder the lady lived so long. If only

Elizabeth could bottle up her friend's faith and prescribe it to herself, rather than worrying.

"Bless you, Mrs. Mary," Elizabeth whispered against Mrs. Mary's ear, her wispy white hair tickling her lips. "You've no idea what an inspiration you are."

She said the last words so low maybe Mrs. Mary didn't hear her. If she had, she'd be fussing that Jesus was the one they needed to look to for inspiration.

As difficult as it was for such a capable, independent woman to accept she needed help, her recent fall had been a wake-up call, not only for her but also for her family. She was getting older, and she needed help, like it or not, because they *needed* her.

Talking of others… Where were they? The house seemed strangely quiet. Not even any children running around. Odd.

Olivia's call ended, and she rejoined them, her face ashen. "That was Dad. Still no sign of Sean."

A chill wove down Elizabeth's spine. "You'd best tell us what happened."

Olivia blew out a heavy breath and perched on an upholstered armchair. "He and David rode out to check on the cattle early this morning, and he… just rode off. His horse came back before lunch, and the men have been out looking for him since then."

Elizabeth's heart raced as the lump in her stomach grew heavier. "I need to join them."

"Wouldn't it be best for you to stay here in case he turns up?"

"That's unlikely, isn't it? It's more likely he's lying in some gully. What if he's hurt? I'm a nurse, so I should go."

Olivia tapped her fingers on her thighs. "I'll call Dad and ask him to come back for you. He's on one of the quad bikes. Most of the others are on horseback because the ground's so wet."

"That'd be great. I was just about to redress Mrs. Mary's wounds."

"I can do it."

At her cousin's voice, Elizabeth spun around. "Stella! Look at you!" She hurried forward and hugged her as Olivia stepped out of the room. "How are you doing?"

"Fine, but I wish this baby would come already."

"First babies usually don't come early."

Stella rubbed her stomach and rolled her eyes. "So everyone keeps telling me. But maybe I got the dates wrong. I feel like she should have come a month ago."

"Every expectant mum feels like that." Elizabeth let out a heavy breath. Although children hadn't been on her radar, with Sean missing, most likely injured, it hit her that not only might they never get married but also she might never become a mum.

Did she want to be a mother? Did she want children?

She needed to ponder that. Stella was obviously excited about it.

Stella patted Elizabeth's arm. "Let me look after Mrs. Mary. I know you're worried about Sean. We'd hoped he'd be found by the time you arrived. Joshua's out looking for him with the others."

Although not a crier, Elizabeth blinked as her eyes burned. She glanced away to get a grip. "Thanks, Stell. I can't believe he just rode off. What was he thinking?"

"I'm not sure." Acting the mother already, Stella straightened out Elizabeth's scrub top.

Elizabeth studied her cousin. Was she hiding something? "What is it? Tell me."

Stella slipped her arm across Elizabeth's shoulders. "Let's have a cup of tea."

That bad, huh? "What about Mrs. Mary?"

"She's asleep. I'll do her dressings when she wakes."

Olivia re-entered the room. "Or I can do them."

Goodness. Where had this caring Olivia come from? Elizabeth tucked stray hairs behind her ear. "Would you? That'd be great."

"It's not a problem." Olivia spread out her hands. "And Dad'll be here in about fifteen minutes."

"Great." Elizabeth managed a smile. "We were just grabbing a cup of tea. Would you like to join us?"

"Thanks, but I'll stay here with Gran."

Wow. Such tenderness in her voice. Olivia was showing another side of herself. Mrs. Mary's fall seemed to have affected everyone.

Everyone except Sean. Mrs. Mary was his grandmother, too. And where was he?

Leaving Olivia with Mrs. Mary, Elizabeth and Stella headed along the hall to the dining room where hot and cold refreshments had been laid out for everyone to help themselves whenever they wanted. No one else was there. Good. Not that she wanted to avoid people. Not at all, but she needed to hear what Stella had to tell her. Joshua and Sean had travelled on the circuit together during their rebellious years, and if anyone knew what was going on with him, Joshua would. Although he and Stella lived at Indigo Downs, the guys still spoke regularly, and Joshua was a good influence on Sean.

So, what had gone wrong?

Holding cups of steaming tea, they settled onto cane rockers on the verandah. Bright summer sunlight splashed along the puddles, creating a blinding patchwork, while children's high-pitched squeals came from the paddock bordering Maggie's vegetable garden.

Stella sipped her tea. "Maggie and Serena are playing with the kids to keep them distracted."

That meant everyone was worried. Elizabeth leaned forward and settled her teacup onto the nearby end table. "Tell me what you know."

Stella drew a long breath. Rubbed her stomach. "He's not been himself for a few weeks, and this morning, he told David he's going back to the circuit." She lifted her gaze and met Elizabeth's. "We don't think he meant it, but he's troubled."

Elizabeth's heart fell. He didn't love her. She averted her gaze as her eyes burned again. She blinked the tears away. She wouldn't cry, even though her heart was breaking.

How could he do this to her?

Stella reached out and squeezed her hand. "He loves you, Liz. He's just scared. That's all."

With her free hand, Elizabeth gripped her armrest. As the cane pressed against her tender palms, the pain coming from somewhere other than her heart grounded her. Yes, deep down, she knew he loved her, and her heart ached for him. If only he could leave his demons behind, once and for all.

Because if he didn't, would she marry him? Could she live

her life with someone who lacked inner strength? She didn't want to go through life picking up Sean's messes.

Maybe she should go travelling with Bree.

She swung her gaze to her cousin's. "I'm thinking of going overseas."

"You?" Stella's eyes widened. "I don't believe it."

Elizabeth could understand that. She'd always said she'd rather see Australia before travelling the world. She shrugged. "Bree's going and invited me along."

"Don't give up on him yet. Maybe this will bring everything to a head."

"He could have waited until after Christmas to ride off. He's going to ruin it for everyone."

Stella squeezed her hand again. "It's all going to work out."

If only Elizabeth was so sure. "He has to be found first."

"Yes, and here's Frank."

Leaving her tea, Elizabeth pushed to her feet. "I'll finish it later." She bent and hugged Stella. "Pray for us?"

"I haven't stopped."

Moments later, Elizabeth was in the quad bike with Frank. "So, where are we headed?"

He levelled a serious expression on her, then revved the machine. "Deadman's Gully."

CHAPTER 6

*H*er heart heavy, Maggie waved as Frank drove by, Elizabeth beside him, clinging to the rail. The last thing they wanted was a Christmas tragedy, but Sean had been missing for eight hours. No one had said anything, but they were all thinking the same, although they were praying for a miracle.

As a cowboy, Sean could survive out there on his own, but not if his horse had thrown him and he'd landed in a raging river. That's what they all feared. The rivers and creeks were swollen and running fast. Frank's first wife drowned while saving Sasha and Caleb from the flooded Ord River—surely, everyone was thinking of that.

As Maggie and Serena kept the kids busy playing in the paddock, she didn't stop praying. Sean had to be found before dark. He had to be.

When Frank heard the news that morning, he'd called the Emergency Services team in Kununurra and put them on alert.

With limited volunteers available and the likelihood that the family would find Sean quickly, he'd told them not to come unless necessary. He did, however, call on their neighbours for help. Stuart McEnaney and Bill Dodds had arrived.

Less than four hours of daylight remained.

With the Emergency Services team since being deployed to another incident, they were on their own.

As the quad disappeared into the distance, an unfamiliar car approached and stopped in front of the homestead. Janella?

Maggie called to Serena. She was playing tiggy with the kids, and despite the situation, warmth surged through Maggie. Seeing her daughter so happy and carefree was wonderful. The transformation in her life was nothing short of a miracle. They did happen, and Maggie clung to that now.

Serena stopped, eyed the car, and gave Maggie a nod before turning to the kids. "Come on, guys. Let's get some lemonade."

"And some gingerbread men?" Oliver asked.

"We can manage that." They'd done Christmas baking with the kids that morning and created gingerbread men in all shapes and sizes. They'd also made a gingerbread house but would keep it until tomorrow to eat.

Right now, who knew what tomorrow would bring? *Please, Lord, not a tragedy.*

"Can we have ice cream as well?" Isobel jumped up and down.

Serena ruffled the girl's hair. "I'm not so sure about that, but we'll see."

"Okay." Issie's acceptance was so typical of her. She was such a good girl.

They crossed the paddock and Maggie's vegetable garden.

Normally, she'd have stopped to pull weeds, check the beans, smell the rosemary, but not today.

She'd called Janella at lunchtime to alert her to the unfolding drama. Although Sasha and Caleb were now in their midteens, they'd never forget the day their grandmother drowned. But they didn't need to know they feared Sean might have met the same fate. Their prayer was that he was out there somewhere, alive. They just had to find him.

Janella, Wade, and the kids were out of the car by the time Maggie's group reached them.

Maggie paused in front of Janella, and as their gazes met, unspoken words passed between them. When Maggie first came to Goddard Downs as Frank's wife, she and Janella bonded despite their age difference. Janella knew what it was like to marry into the family. Not that anyone was hostile to Maggie, but she had big shoes to fill. She'd never take Esther's place. She'd never be Julian, Olivia, and Joshua's mother. She'd never be the family matriarch. And yet, she couldn't think of anywhere she'd rather be. This was her home. Her family. And although Janella now lived in Darwin, Goddard Downs would always be her home, as well. And she'd be feeling the emotion of the situation just as much as anyone else.

Maggie put her arms out, and Janella walked into them. "So good to see you, Nell." Maggie's voice caught as she held her friend close.

"And you. Is there any word?"

Maggie shook her head as she eased from the hug. "Not yet." She kept her voice low. "What did you tell the kids?"

"The truth."

"Oh."

"There was no use sugar-coating it. They would have sensed it immediately."

They *were* clever kids. She gave her friend another squeeze. "You're right."

Janella motioned for the kids and Wade to join them.

Maggie smiled at Wade before drawing Caleb and Sasha into her arms. "You've grown so tall, Caleb. What's your mum been feeding you?"

He ducked his head and kicked his feet in the mucky gravel. "Just the usual."

She chuckled, tugged at his sleeve, then grabbed Sasha's hand. She'd celebrated her fifteenth birthday last month and now wore eye make-up, and her once-heavy eyebrows were thinned and shaped. "And look at you, Sash. You're so grown up."

It happened so quickly. Not long ago, Sasha was an unsophisticated preteen, only interested in baking and playing the piano. No doubt she'd now be interested in boys and magazines.

And Janella had undergone a transformation, too. Julian would have been so proud of her. She now wore clothes that highlighted her curvy figure instead of hiding it under over-sized shirts and dresses. Her brows, too, were shaped and not as heavy as they'd been. She'd matured into a beautiful, confident woman, comfortable in her own skin, just like Julian had always wanted for her. She now owned one of the most successful restaurants in Darwin. Praise God she'd taken that step of faith and gone to culinary school.

And she'd met this super handsome man. Wade.

Maggie approached him. "So nice to see you." She reached

up and hugged him. He wasn't overly tall. Perhaps five ten. And a warm smile accentuated his kind face.

"It's good to be here. I've heard so much about the place." As she released him, his gaze wandered to the homestead and then to the paddocks stretching into the distance.

"I'm sure you have." Unable to imagine being anywhere else, Maggie breathed in deeply the earth-scented air, the scent of home. "I hope you'll feel at home here. How was the drive?"

"Long." He pinched the bridge of his nose with two fingers, tension evident in his shoulders. "And we came through a heavy storm."

Maggie winced. "It came through here not long ago."

"You must be worried. Can I do anything to help?"

She managed a grateful smile. "The last thing you'd want to do after such a long drive is join the search. The men are all out there. We're praying Sean will be found soon."

Caleb jerked his chin up. "I'd like to help. I know the station like no one else does."

"Oh, sweetie. That's so kind of you." Maggie rubbed his thin arm. "Grandpa would have loved you to help, but you just missed him. He and Elizabeth left on the quad."

"I'll go after him. Is the bike in the shed?"

"I think so." Frank and Caleb had rebuilt an old motorcycle when Caleb was twelve and still grieving for his grandmother.

"Can I, Mum?" He shuffled his feet as if unable to keep still, his expression almost desperate.

Janella drew a long breath, then gave a nod. "Yes, but please be careful."

"I will." He spun towards the shed, sprinted a few steps,

then pivoted back to them, walking backwards as he spoke. "Which way did they go?"

Maggie bit her bottom lip. She wasn't liking this. If anything happened to him, she'd never forgive herself. But she could understand his determination. "They took the lower track, and they're heading for Deadman's Gully. The others are searching higher up. If you're going to catch them, you'd best hurry. But don't take any risks."

"I won't. And thank you." He sprinted off down the track to the shed.

"Keep your phone on," Janella shouted after him.

He raised a hand in a backward wave. Although phone reception was dodgy away from the homestead, having a phone provided a level of comfort because occasionally a weak signal popped up.

There'd been no response from Sean's phone, and its last known position wasn't far from where he'd left David early that morning. There was no sign of him there, so he must be in a black spot.

They'd all prayed that spot wasn't a swollen creek.

Maggie tugged at Janella's sleeve. "Come inside and freshen up. You must be tired after that long trip."

"Thanks. It wasn't too bad. Sharing the driving helped." As Janella looked up at Wade, love shone in her dark eyes.

He draped his arm around her shoulders. "There were three drivers."

Maggie frowned, and then the penny dropped. "Caleb. I forgot he had his learner driver's permit." Her gaze shifted to Wade's Range Rover. "You let him drive your car?"

He nodded. "He's a good kid and a good driver. I wouldn't let many of the kids at school drive my car. He's an exception."

He had that right. Caleb *was* a good kid. Losing his grandmother and his father could have made him go off the rails, but he'd grown through adversity. Giving his heart to the Lord at age thirteen had helped him, and having Frank as his mentor during those troubling years had made all the difference. And it seemed his peers looked up to him because he'd been elected school captain for the following year at the prestigious Darwin school where Wade worked as a student liaison officer.

"I'll grab the bags and follow you in." Wade headed to the boot.

"I'll help." Sasha followed him.

Maggie leaned closer to Janella and lowered her voice. "Sasha seems to like him."

Janella linked their arms. "They get on well. I was worried at first, but she's warmed to him. He understands kids, and he understands that she and Caleb are still grieving for Julian, so he doesn't ask too much of them. He's just there for them."

"That's wonderful, Nell. I'm so happy for you." Maggie faced her friend, quirking a brow as they strolled towards the steps. "So…?"

Janella's olive skin turned a pretty pink, and then she beamed. "He's asked me to marry him."

Maggie let out a squeal. "And you said yes?"

"Shh." Janella put a finger to her lips. "We haven't told anyone yet."

"I won't say anything. Do the kids know?"

"Yes. They're the only ones."

"And they're okay with it?"

Janella beamed. "I wouldn't have agreed if they weren't."

As they reached the top of the steps, Olivia came, and her face lit up. "Janella! You made it. So good to see you. Come here." Laughing, she embraced her sister-in-law.

The door opened again, and Mrs. Mary hobbled out.

"Gran!" Janella let go of Olivia and bent down to hug Mrs. Mary. "You're looking great."

Drawing back, Mrs. Mary snorted. "The others don't think so. They're mollycoddling me, keeping me tucked away inside like I'm about to die."

"They're just concerned about you." Janella patted her gran's arms, ever so gently. "That's all."

"Perhaps, but I'm not going to stay inside the whole time, wrapped in cottonwool. I want to see the station in its entirety, not just the inside of the homestead."

"I'm sure they've got things planned for you."

"I hope so, but first, Sean has to be found. But enough of that. How are you, dear? And how's that new man of yours? I've heard a lot about him."

"Would you like to meet him?"

"I'd love to." She peered around Janella. "He looks handsome."

Janella's face pinked again. "He is. But he's also clever."

When Mrs. Mary stumbled, Janella grabbed her. Stabilised her. "Let's go inside and sit down."

Mrs. Mary tutted. "If you insist. But introduce me first."

"Sure." Janella motioned for Wade to join them. He carried the bags up the steps, set them down, and then stood beside her.

"Gran, this is Wade Johnson. Wade, this is Mary Goddard, Julian's grandmother, and the matriarch of the family."

Mrs. Mary's gaze travelled over him before she held out her hand. "Welcome to the family."

Maggie's eyebrows shot up. But Wade seemed to be taking it all in his stride.

"Thank you. It's a pleasure to meet you, and I'm excited to be here."

"No need to put on airs and graces. No pretences here. What you see is what you get. Just do the right thing by this girl. She's been through a lot."

"I intend to."

"Good. Now, who's this young woman behind you?"

Maggie slipped her arm around her granddaughter's waist. The girl had gone bright red. "It's Sasha, Mary. Don't you recognise her?"

Mrs. Mary peered at her. "What have you done to your face, girl?"

"Gran!" Olivia's voice was loud and firm. "She's a city girl now, and she wears make-up. But she's still our Sasha."

"I'm sorry, luv. You look so grown up, I didn't recognise you. But you shouldn't bother with all that stuff. You're beautiful just the way God made you."

When Maggie gave Sasha a gentle nudge, she stepped forward and kissed Mrs. Mary on the cheek. "Thanks, Grandma Mary. And so are you."

Mrs. Mary chuckled, her old eyes twinkling. "I can see God also gave you charm. Now, help me back to my chair, will you? That's a dear."

"Sure." Sasha gripped Mrs. Mary's elbow and walked slowly inside with her while everyone else followed. As she reached her chair, Mrs. Mary frowned. "Where's Caleb?"

"Looking for Sean."

"Oh." She eased into her chair. "We should pray for that boy. He needs to be found so we can all enjoy Christmas."

"Good idea. Let's do that." Perching on the wide arm of Mrs. Mary's armchair, Maggie took the dear lady's withered hand in hers. "Let's pray, shall we?"

She bowed her head. "Heavenly Father, we come before You now, asking for a miracle. Lord, You know where Sean is, and so we ask that You guide those looking for him to that place. May they find him, and may he be brought home safely so we can all celebrate Jesus' birthday together, as a family. Lord, You know the deep emotion we're all experiencing right now. It's so easy to slip into negative thinking and think the worst, but we ask for Your mercy and grace. Please bring Sean home. In Jesus' precious name, we pray. Amen."

"Yes, Lord," Mrs. Mary continued. "He needs to come home so he can propose to Elizabeth. I pray that whatever happened to him has knocked some sense into him. Let him realise what he'll miss out on if he doesn't ask that girl to marry him. Just do it, Lord. Don't dillydally. In Jesus' name. Amen."

Maggie stifled a chuckle. Just as well God had a sense of humour. He must have a soft spot for this elderly woman who'd loved and served Him her entire life. Mrs. Mary didn't need to stand on pretence before Him. Instead, she spoke to God as if they were best buddies.

But Maggie doubted she could ever talk to God like that.

Although she was saved and knew He loved her, she didn't deserve His love. He was God, the creator and sustainer of the universe, and she needed to respect Him. Maybe one day she'd talk to Him like Mrs. Mary did, but for now, she'd ask politely and with reverence for Sean's safe return.

After they finished praying, Olivia showed Janella, Wade, and Sasha to their rooms while Maggie remained on the armrest of Mrs. Mary's chair. Serena had taken the younger children to the back room for lemonade and gingerbread men.

"So, dear, what's your take on Wade? Is he a keeper?"

Maggie let out a slow breath. "I think so. Janella seems happy, and the kids like him."

Mrs. Mary adjusted her position in the chair. "Sometimes I forget Julian's gone. But you know what? Even though he was my grandson, I wished I could've put him over my knee and spanked him. He was too full of himself at times."

Holding her tongue, Maggie draped an arm around her friend's shoulder and tucked their heads together until Mrs. Mary's wispy hair tickled her cheek and her rosewood scent teased her nostrils. That trait had resulted in his untimely death. But God had wrought good out of that sad event. Freed from living under Julian's shadow, Joshua had come into his own and grown into a responsible, mature man of God. And now he was about to become a father. Janella had also stepped out of her comfort zone and developed her career as a restaurateur. And God had blessed her with a new love.

"We all forget at times." Maggie grabbed a paisley cushion and tucked it behind Mrs. Mary's back. "But yes, Wade's a keeper."

"Good. I hope I live long enough to see them married, along

with that grandson of mine and my nurse. She's a keeper, too. He's a fool if he doesn't see that."

"We all think the same. I'm hoping for two engagement announcements this Christmas."

Mrs. Mary's eyes twinkled. "That would be nice."

CHAPTER 7

*S*ean had to be somewhere. Clinging to the quad's handrail and perched on the edge of her seat, Elizabeth kept her eyes peeled as Frank navigated the deep ruts and rocks the rain had exposed.

Sean could be anywhere. How far had he ridden before being thrown from his horse? Because of the rain, they couldn't track his path. Even the local Indigenous trackers would have trouble. Working backwards from the time his horse returned to the homestead, they'd estimated he could have ridden many kilometres from where he'd left David. Unless the horse had stayed with him before returning.

And where was his phone?

Elizabeth glanced at her own. She'd called him like a hundred times. Grr. No signal. She let out a groan. They should all have satellite phones. It was ridiculous they didn't.

As Frank rounded a corner, she squealed when the quad

tipped onto two wheels before thudding back to four. She tightened her grip and inhaled deeply.

"Sorry about that." Frank grimaced, but a grin twitched at its edges. He'd have enjoyed the ride if their mission wasn't so serious.

Reaching the fast-flowing creek, he parked on a flat area. "We'll need to get out and walk."

She jumped out and peered along the creek. No sign of Sean. The water gushed over and around rocks and swirled in an eddy. Above its noise, she heard what sounded like a motorcycle. "Can you hear that?"

He frowned. "Hear what?"

"A motorcycle."

"Maybe. But I don't know who it'd be. Everyone else is searching lower down."

The sound grew louder. Yep, a motorcycle soon stopped beside the quad.

"Caleb!" Frank beamed as his grandson alighted and strode towards him. He gave him a bear hug and held him at arm's length. "What are you doing here?"

"Helping to find Sean."

"Well, I didn't expect to see you, but it's a nice surprise. We're running out of time before dark sets in. I've got a hunch he's here somewhere. Don't ask me why. I just have."

"Then let's get started. Which way do you want me to go?"

"How about you and Elizabeth go downstream, and I'll go up."

Caleb angled his head. "I don't want to be rude. But I should go up, and you and Elizabeth go down. I'm young and fit."

Frank pursed his lips. "If we weren't in such a situation, I'd take offence, but you're right. Take this flare. Set it off if you find him. I'll set one off if we do."

"Roger that." Caleb checked his watch. "Shall we meet back here in an hour if we don't find him?"

Elizabeth didn't know Caleb that well, but she remembered him being a quiet boy who lacked confidence. Attending school in Darwin must've changed that.

"Sounds like a plan." Frank tipped his watch into view, then held his other hand over it to shield it from the glare. "Half past four, back here if we don't find him." He slapped Caleb on the back. "Take care, son. This water's dangerous."

Of course, he knew. She wasn't around when his grandmother drowned, but she'd heard the story. This would be a real challenge for Caleb. All the more reason to pray for a positive outcome. Elizabeth wouldn't consider any other.

Caleb headed upstream while she and Frank headed down, clambering over rocks, peering into the eddies and under the branches and logs wedged at odd angles. Dappled sunlight sliced through the trees, and at any other time, the sheer beauty of the place would've awed her. But today, she had no time to dawdle.

They stopped for a breather on a flat-topped rock. "Do you think he's here somewhere?" She winced at the doubt in her voice. Why would Sean have ridden here? It was no place to take a horse.

Frank removed his cap and ran a hand over his damp hair. "Maybe I got it wrong. I thought I heard a little voice inside me telling me to come here. But it could've just been wishful thinking."

"But maybe it wasn't. We should keep going, just in case."

Turning to clamber off the rock, she stopped in her tracks. Was that orange smoke through the trees? "Look, Frank. Is that Caleb's flare?"

Frank followed the direction of her pointed hand. "Well, I'll be. It sure is."

In her haste to get to him, she almost tumbled down the rock.

"Take it easy, Liz. We don't want two casualties."

Good point. She slowed and took careful steps, but her heart raced. She prayed Sean was alive. How awful for Caleb if he wasn't.

How awful for her.

How awful for them all.

She gulped. He *had* to be alive. Surely, God wouldn't let him die now. Not now when she knew she loved him and she'd wait a lifetime, if that's how long it took, for him to propose.

There was no one else she'd rather spend her life with.

SEAN GULPED FOR AIR. He had to time it right, because the water lapped his chin, and if he got it wrong, he'd get a mouthful of water. But what did it matter? He only had minutes left. No way could he free his foot before the water covered his head.

Then, just when he thought he'd never be found, Caleb appeared.

Too bad it was too late.

Caleb ripped his shirt off and waded into the water.

"Don't, mate. It's too dangerous." Sean's voice gargled as water gushed into his mouth.

"I can't let you drown."

"You'll drown with me if you get washed away."

Caleb waded in further. "I have to try."

Sean closed his eyes. He couldn't watch. How would Uncle Frank handle it if Caleb drowned trying to rescue him? Sean wouldn't be missed, but Caleb? He had his whole life ahead of him. He was the future of Goddard Downs. Not Sean. Nobody would miss him. Not even Elizabeth.

Tears streamed down his cheeks and mingled with the water.

He'd been such a fool. Why had he let his father's words get to him? He shouldn't have listened. He should've accepted what God said about him. That he was a precious, much-loved child.

Was God waiting to welcome him now? What would He say about him? Not 'well done, good and faithful servant', that was for sure. More like, 'you should have trusted Me'.

He blacked out and then came to. This was it. The moment was coming. He'd heard drowning was a peaceful way to go. He'd find out any second if that were true.

ELIZABETH SCRAMBLED over the rocks as fast as she could. She had to get to Sean. Frank followed, but the gap between them was widening. Should she wait for him? What if he had another heart attack trying to keep up? No, she couldn't think like that. She had to push on. Every second was crucial. Sean's life could be in the balance.

Lord, please watch over Sean. Thank You that Caleb found him. And watch over Frank.

Her chest was heaving by the time she reached the quad. But she had to keep going. Frank had estimated Caleb released the flare about a hundred metres upstream. It didn't sound far, but the jagged rocks and rushing water would make it slow going.

She looked behind for Frank. She could just see him in the distance. "Frank, are you okay?" Although she shouted, the rushing water drowned out her voice.

He gave a thumbs up.

She pointed upstream. "I'll keep going."

At his nod, she pushed on, shouting for Caleb and for Sean every few metres. It was slow going. The rocks grew larger and slipperier. How had Sean ended up here?

A boulder the size of a cabin loomed ahead. She should go around it. Climbing over it would be foolish. But how? Dense scrub could be a brick wall. She'd wade through the water. That'd be best. She had to be careful. Hang onto something the whole time. If she lost her footing... No, again, she couldn't think like that. She'd be super cautious.

Lord, please help me do this. Keep me safe.

Her heart thumped as she entered the swollen creek. Was this foolishness? Water rushed around her, its force almost pushing her back. She forged on, staying as close to the edge as she could, using the rocks to steady her.

Her foot slipped, and she went under. Heart pounding, with water swirling all around her, she struggled to regain her footing. This was crazy. But she couldn't give up now. She had to get to Sean.

Back on her feet, she pushed on. Rounding the boulder, she half swam, half waded until she clutched for the safety of the rocks.

Panting, she sucked in air.

Had she been mad?

She could have drowned.

What an idiot.

How would Frank get around the boulder? "Lord, please look after him."

She scrambled to her feet. "Sean! Caleb!"

She waited. Listened. Nothing.

No. There was something. She was sure of it. A voice? Or was she imagining it?

She pushed on. Encountered another boulder. This time, she scrambled through the bushes. A few cuts and scratches were neither here nor there.

She called again. Nothing.

But then, as she rounded a bend, there they were.

Praise God. Tears seared her eyes. "Sean! I'm here."

His head was only just above the water, and Caleb stood behind him, holding his chin up.

Was Sean unconscious?

No, his eyes opened. Phew.

"Sean!"

When his gaze turned to her, her heart melted. This was her man, and he needed her.

"I'm coming." She hurried on.

Before she waded into the water, Caleb stopped her. "We need rope. Or a strong vine."

"I'll see what I can find."

There wouldn't be any rope, so a vine would have to suffice. She headed into the dense foliage and came face to face with Frank. "How did you get here so fast?"

"I came along the track."

Wait? There was a track? She'd risked her life needlessly? Whatever. "Caleb needs a rope. Do you have any?"

"No, but I have a knife." He proceeded to cut a long section of vine, metres of it, which she coiled up as best she could.

They hurried to the creek.

Her heart clenched. Water was rushing over Sean's face. Only Caleb holding his head up was allowing him to grab an occasional breath. But for how long?

Six inches taller than Sean, Caleb had his head clear. Praise God.

"We need to get out there." Panic surged inside her.

"Caleb got to him just in time." Even Frank looked panicked. "The water's rising."

"What should we do?"

"I'll tie the vine to a tree, and we'll wade out. Between the three of us, we should be able to get him out."

Good thing Frank kept a calm head. She'd have launched herself into the flow and been washed away.

They found a tree, and he tied the vine around it. Then they waded into the water, using the vine to steady themselves.

The water rushed around her. Her foot slipped on a rock. She went under. Pulled herself up.

When they reached Caleb and Sean, she pressed her lips to Sean's head. "You're going to be okay."

She couldn't touch bottom. She clung to Frank and the vine he'd tied around himself.

"Why can't Sean move?" She peered into the water.

Caleb's jaw was rigid. "His foot's wedged between rocks. If you two can hold him, I'll go down and try to free it."

"I'll help. I'm a good swimmer." And she'd done a survival training course.

"Grandpa, take over for me. Hold his head up. He can only just breathe."

Frank shifted into position.

Elizabeth met Sean's gaze through the water, his eyes dark and filled with fear. "We'll get you out. I promise." She kissed him long and hard, breathing air into his mouth.

"Are you ready?" Caleb asked her.

With a nod, she took a deep breath and dove, clinging to Sean's legs to avoid being washed away.

The murky water stung her eyes, but she had to keep them open.

Caleb pointed to the top rock pinning down Sean's foot. Together, they worked at raising it.

This had to work. Sean's life depended on it.

Lord, give us strength.

A Bible verse came to her. "Truly I tell you, if you have faith as small as a mustard seed, you can say to this mountain, 'Move from here to there,' and it will move. Nothing will be impossible for you."

Was her faith strong enough?

Lord, help us move this rock. I have faith.

The rock eased up, and Sean's foot moved.

Just a bit more.

Her lungs burned as she put all her effort into lifting that sucker.

And then his foot was free.

Frank lost his footing, and the current swept him and Sean away.

No!

She clung to Caleb and swam to the surface. Gulped some air. Caleb held her as he steadied his footing. Her heart raced as fast as the water swirling around them—the water carrying Frank and Sean around the bend.

Would the vine hold them, or would they be swept away? Not far downstream was a ravine. Deadman's Gully.

"What do we do?" she shouted over the rushing water, panic gripping her throat. They were close to the opposite bank. "Do we get out and try to catch Frank and Sean on foot? Or let the water carry us downstream?"

"We'll go after them. Stay close." Caleb held out his hand. She took it, and they launched into the fast-flowing water.

People died in rapids like these. But she wouldn't let herself think like that.

CHAPTER 8

*M*aggie shielded her eyes from the sun and checked her phone. She'd tried calling Frank several times in the last hour, but each time, it went straight to voicemail. He was still out of range.

With her concern growing, she paced the soggy grass beside the homestead.

What if they didn't find Sean before dark?

And why hadn't Frank taken his satellite phone? She'd gotten him a new one for his birthday, but he remained blasé about the need for it, as if carrying flares was enough. Ridiculous. It was the twenty-first century, not the nineteenth.

She and the other adults had done their best to hide their concern from the children. It was Christmas Eve, after all. After Janella, Wade, and Sasha settled in, they all played a game of backyard cricket on the grassed area alongside the homestead. Even Stella joined in. Maggie had suggested she sit out and watch, but she'd insisted. "I'm fine. Physical activity might hurry the baby along."

Maggie just nodded. What if the baby came tonight and they were still searching for Sean? Although the baby would come when it was good and ready and in God's timing, what if it did come tonight? They were three hours from the nearest hospital. And it was Christmas Eve. But then, Mary and Joseph had no hospital, no doctor, and no place to stay. How awful it must have been for them, and yet, there in that lowly stable, surrounded by farm animals, Mary gave birth to a healthy baby boy. The Son of God. God was with them, as He would be with Stella and Joshua when she went into labour, whenever that might be. Even if it were tonight. So no use worrying about it.

"Hey, Mum. The ball just whizzed past you. Didn't you see it?" Serena stood with her hands on her hips.

"Sorry. I was miles away." Maggie jogged after the ball, snagged it from the ground metres behind her, and then threw it to Janella, who was bowling.

She had to concentrate. She couldn't do anything to help find Sean other than pray, which she'd been doing all day.

Isobel was batting. Olivia stood behind her, helping her swing when the ball approached. She missed, and her lower lip came out in a pout. "I told you I can't play cricket."

"You can. You just need to concentrate." Olivia repositioned her daughter's hands on the bat. "Hold it lower down and keep your eye on the ball. Swing to meet it."

Easier said than done. Maggie would have no chance of connecting the bat with the ball, not even the wider one they were using, although she'd give it her best shot on her turn.

Janella bowled again. This time, Isobel's bat connected, and the ball came straight for Maggie.

Oh.

Should she try to catch it? If by some miracle she managed to, Isobel would be out.

Caught on the full.

Could Maggie do that to the little girl?

She made a fumbled attempt, but missed.

No one would have expected her to catch it anyway, so it was all good.

Isobel made a run for the opposite wicket, beaming when she reached it without being caught out.

Wade was umpiring, and he held up his hand, indicating she was safe.

The game continued until Serena announced a break for lemonade and watermelon.

"Gingerbread men, too?" Oliver's face was flushed. His soft, blond curls dangling to one side, he looked up at his mother with such an impish grin Maggie wouldn't have been able to deny him.

But Serena did. "No, we're having watermelon."

His lip came out, and he folded his arms. "I want ginger-bread men."

"You can't always have what you want, little man." Serena stayed firm. "Besides, you kids ate them all earlier."

"We can make more."

"We could, but we're going on a scavenger hunt after our break."

"What's a–a?"

"A scavenger hunt?"

Oliver nodded.

"It's when we have to find things from a list of clues."

"Like we did at Easter?"

"Just like we did at Easter."

His little face lit up, and he raced ahead to catch William and Isobel. "Guess what? We're having an Easter hunt."

William looked at him with disdain. "We can't have an Easter hunt, silly. It's Christmas."

Olivia hurried to join the children. "William! Be nice to Oliver. He's only little, and he doesn't understand."

"Sorry, Mum."

"Apology accepted. But when we do the hunt, you might have to help him."

William rolled his eyes. "Okay."

Maggie hid a chuckle. They were just like Jeremy and Serena at that age.

Serena went inside and returned with a jug of lemonade and a tray of sliced watermelon Maggie had grown in her garden. Serena placed both on a table under a shade tree.

The kids hovered around like bees in a springtime flower garden. Serena put her hand up. "There's plenty here. Take a piece each and, once you're finished, come back for another. Grandma Maggie will pour the lemonade."

But as Maggie stepped forward, her phone rang, and her heart raced.

Had Sean been found?

She fumbled it from her pocket, then frowned at the contact on the screen. Not Frank or any of the searchers. Letting out a sigh, she swiped to answer.

"Hey, Maggie!" her sister in Darwin sang out. "Just calling to wish you and Frank a happy Christmas. I hope all's well?"

Maggie took a deep breath. Her younger sister had never been in favour of her moving to Goddard Downs, claiming Maggie would go crazy in such a backwater—and she'd have to be crazy already to throw away her job to live on a cattle station.

But Maggie never made a better decision, apart from renewing her faith. And marrying Frank, of course.

She tucked some hair behind her ear, motioned for Serena to take over pouring the lemonade, and moved away from the table. "Hey, Denise. Happy Christmas to you and Derek as well. Are you dining at Mirages again this year?"

With no children or extended family nearby, the couple often indulged in an expensive Christmas meal at Mirages on Mindil, the swankiest restaurant in the city offering amazing views across Fannie Bay.

Maggie and Frank enjoyed dining there whenever they were in Darwin, but she couldn't imagine not spending Christmas with her children and grandchildren.

"I couldn't imagine dining anywhere else."

"Oh well. Enjoy it."

"I guess you'll be cooking everything for yourselves."

"Absolutely. We all pull together, and it's fun."

"To each, his own, I guess."

"Hey, we've got a situation here, and I need to get off the phone."

"A situation. What kind of situation?"

"Sean's missing."

"Sean?"

Right. Denise never listened when Maggie spoke of her new family. "Frank's nephew."

"Oh. The one he appointed manager?"

Huh, maybe she did listen. *Sorry for judging her, Lord!* "That's him."

"He sounded like a bit of a deadbeat."

Well, apparently, she wasn't the only one being judgmental. Maggie clenched her fists. "He's changed."

"But he's disappeared." Denise tsked. "Doesn't sound like he's changed that much."

"I must get off the phone in case Frank calls. I'll call you after Christmas, okay?"

"Okay. Whatever. Enjoy your home-cooked meal."

"We will."

After Maggie ended the call, she pressed her phone to her chest and stared across the paddock. She hadn't meant to be rude. It was so unlike her, but with Sean still missing, how could she engage in small talk? *It would be different, Lord, if Denise was ready to talk about something important.*

"We have almost nothing in common anymore," she whispered the admission, but the words didn't hurt as much as they should. Her life was here in this amazing place with Frank and his family.

And Sean was part of that family.

How could they contemplate celebrating Christmas without him?

Lord, we have to find him. Please guide Frank and the others to wherever he is. Keep them all safe and return them in time to celebrate Christmas together. I ask this in Jesus' precious name. Amen.

"Grandma Maggie, why are you crying?" Isobel tugged her hand.

Crying? She didn't know she was. Maggie dabbed her eyes. "The sun's in my eyes. That's all."

But it wasn't all, not by a long shot. It was Christmas Eve, and one of their own was missing.

But even with her heart heavy, she had to trust God to bring him—and Frank—home.

She ruffled Isobel's silky brown hair. "How's that watermelon?"

"It's good! Do you want a piece?"

"I'd love one."

And then her phone rang again. This time, her heart rate skittered as she swiped to answer Frank.

Lord, please let it be good news.

CHAPTER 9

*E*lizabeth gasped for air as the current carried her. Her only comfort was that Caleb was beside her.

How far would they go before they found Frank and Sean? The vine must have snapped, or they would have come across them already. She tried not to think about the ten-metre drop ahead. Could Sean survive these rapids after coming so close to drowning? He was strong, but the physical effort to keep his head above water for so long may have taken its toll. She prayed that wasn't the case.

She tumbled around a bend. A fallen tree lay across the creek, and Sean and Frank were clinging to it as the water rushed underneath it. Hallelujah.

She readied herself. This could hurt.

As the tree neared, she reached up, grabbed it, and stopped.

Phew. Caleb stopped beside her, grinned, and gave the thumbs up. "That was cool."

Cool? Her chest heaved. "I could think of other words."

And then her gaze met Sean's. He was alive! Clinging to the tree, she caught her breath before monkeying along to him. "Am I glad to see you."

His eyes filled. "Not as glad as I am to see you. I thought I was a goner."

She inhaled. What must have been going through his mind she couldn't begin to imagine. "You've got Frank to thank for finding you. He had a feeling you were here somewhere."

"Seems I wasn't meant to die."

She nodded. "Seems that way."

"Hey, let's get out of here." Frank motioned for them to follow him to the bank.

Sean moved slowly. He was in pain. Not surprising—his ankle would be cut and bruised. At least he had his foot. At one stage, she'd considered amputation.

How he would have coped, she wasn't sure.

Praise God, it hadn't come to that.

They reached the bank, and Sean collapsed face first into the mud. She knelt beside him and stroked his head as her heart overflowed. "Thank You for saving him, Lord."

Frank crouched beside her. "We won't get the quad down here. We'll have to carry him."

Sean raised his head. "I can walk."

"No, you can't!" What was he thinking? She held up a hand. "Caleb and I can carry him."

"You think I'm too old?" Frank arched a brow.

"No, but we're younger. And Maggie wouldn't want you having another heart attack." Had she said too much? Frank was touchy about his heart condition. A man who'd been so fit and active hated being told to limit his activities. But it was for his own good.

"You win. I'll go ahead and clear the way."

"Great. That'll help. How strong are you feeling, Caleb?"

"Never stronger."

"Good." She rubbed shaky fingers on her thighs. Not that she thought her wet scrubs could dry them, but to stop their trembling. "We should carry Sean between us. He can drape an arm over each of our shoulders and put whatever weight he feels comfortable with on the ground."

"I can walk." Sean pushed to his knees, but then flopped back down. "I guess not."

"We'll carry you. You've been through an ordeal." She stroked the back of his head again.

"Guess I can't argue."

She wobbled to her feet, more shaken than she'd admit, and then she and Caleb lifted Sean to his. Frank helped Sean put his arms around their shoulders, then went ahead.

They walked for half an hour, taking breaks to catch their breath as they navigated past boulders and logs. But the quad and the bike were on the creek's other side. They'd need to cross again. Great.

She and Caleb lowered Sean to the ground.

Frank walked to the water's edge and studied the creek bed. "We can cross here. It's waist deep and slower."

She joined him. "Are you sure?"

"There's no option."

That wasn't an answer, but he was right. With no signal, they couldn't call for help. At least Frank's phone still worked, thanks to his waterproof case. He'd get a signal further up the track, but that was of no use right now.

The other searchers were too far away to see a flare. Nope. They had to cross.

"Okay. Let's do this." She returned to Sean and Caleb. Sean was sitting with his legs flat on the ground, his boot off. His ankle was a mess.

"Is it sore?"

Stupid question. Of course, it was sore.

"Yeah, a bit." He rubbed his calf muscle.

"As soon as we get back, I'll attend to it."

Frank joined them. "There's a first-aid kit in the quad."

"Wonderful." She'd have clapped if she had the energy. "The sooner we can get it cleaned up and bandaged, the better."

"So, what are we waiting for?" Sean attempted to get to his feet.

She bent down. "Let me help you."

"Thanks." He gave a smile that warmed her heart. Perhaps his near-death experience had made him see things differently. Perhaps they still did have a future together. She hoped so.

With Caleb on Sean's other side, they helped him up.

"I'll lead the way." Frank waded into the water.

Again, he was right. It wasn't flowing as fast here. Soon, they sloshed up the far bank.

Frank opened the box on the quad's back carrier and handed Elizabeth the first-aid kit before pulling out a space blanket and wrapping it around Sean.

Despite the hot and humid day, his teeth were chattering, and his lips had turned blue.

They needed to get him to the homestead and into a warm bath.

She cleaned and dressed the wound. Then she climbed in the back of the four-seater, sitting behind Sean, her hand on his shoulder as Caleb rode ahead on the bike.

When they reached the track's highest point, they stopped, and Frank called Maggie. "We've got him, luv. Run a bath, will you? And tell the others."

CHAPTER 10

*M*aggie pressed her phone to her chest. Sean had been found, and he was okay. What an amazing answer to prayer. *Thank You, Lord. This is wonderful.*

She took a moment before rejoining the group at the table. The children had devoured the watermelon and were now running around again. Such boundless energy, unaffected by the heat. What would it be like to be a kid again?

She shared the news with the others.

Now they could celebrate Christmas properly. With Sean's whereabouts unknown, they planned to cancel the Christmas Eve gathering with the neighbours.

But now? They could proceed. She rubbed her hands together. "Okay. We need to get dinner ready for tonight."

With Patty off over the holiday period, they didn't have a designated cook.

Janella waved. "I'm happy to do it."

"I thought you'd want a break." Hands on her hips, Maggie eyed her dear friend.

"I'm happiest when I'm cooking, you know that. Besides, Sasha and Wade can help."

Wade slipped an arm across Janella's shoulders. "I'll be glad to."

Maggie smiled. He seemed like a nice man.

"So long as you're sure. We're planning a barbecue, but not only for us. We've invited the neighbours."

"How many are we talking?"

"Not many. About fifty." Maybe if she said it quickly it wouldn't sound a big deal. Fifty people *were* a lot to cook for. "Frank opened the invitation to everyone. You know what he's like."

"It's okay. I'm used to cooking for a crowd." Janella winked.

"We'll all help. Everything's cut for the salads, they just need assembling, but we need to wrap the potatoes and get the meat out."

"Just as well there's a ready supply."

"Absolutely. And after dinner, we're having a short service and carols by candlelight. I'm so glad it's all going to happen. The kids would have been so upset if we'd cancelled it. They've been practicing their songs and Bible readings all week."

"We'd best get started, then." Janella rubbed her hands together as if copying Maggie's previous let's-get-at-it gesture.

"I'll look after the kids," Serena said.

"Thanks, sweetheart."

"No problem." Serena winked. "Best not to inflict my cooking on anyone."

Maggie couldn't agree more. Holding silent, she smiled as Serena chased after Oliver, who was squealing with delight.

Then Maggie headed inside. While putting an apron on, she stilled. She hadn't seen Stella for a while. Maybe the cricket game had been too much for her and she'd gone in for a rest.

"I'll be right back. I'm going to check on Stella."

"No problem. She looks like she's ready to pop." Janella surveyed the kitchen that had been her domain for years.

Exactly why Maggie didn't want Stella playing cricket.

In the living room, Mrs. Mary had dozed off, and her chin was touching her chest.

No Stella.

She and Joshua were staying in one of the cabins. She must be there.

Hurrying outside, Maggie crossed the yard, wove through her vegetable garden, and headed towards the row of cabins they mainly used for paying guests. Joshua and Stella were staying in the closest one.

A Christmas wreath hung on the door, and tinsel decorated the railing. Stella had been busy. Maggie walked up the steps and tapped on the door. "Stella, are you there?"

No answer.

She tapped again, this time a little louder.

Still no answer.

She pulled out her phone, found Stella's number, and called it. It went to voicemail. Great, keyed up after the day, she couldn't stop imagining the worst.

Lord, I don't know where she is, but You do. Please help me find her and help me not to be so anxious.

As she turned to descend the stairs, the door opened, and a

bleary-eyed Stella stood there. "Maggie. I thought I heard a knock. I was just taking a nap, sorry."

Oh no. "I'm so *so* sorry." Maggie pressed a hand to her heart. "I didn't mean to wake you. I was concerned when I couldn't find you."

"I told Serena I was taking a nap. I should have told you, too. I'm sorry."

"*I* should have checked with the others before racing off." Maggie stepped forward and squeezed Stella's arm. "How are you doing?"

"I'm fine." Stella's thin shoulders drooped. "A little uncomfortable, though."

"Can I get you anything?"

Fanning herself with a hand, Stella slumped against the doorjamb. "Everything's unpacked, and I've put the decorations up."

"I can see that." Maggie jiggled a bell on the door wreath. "The cabin looks Christmassy."

"I love Christmas." Stella's face lit up, but then fell. "I almost forgot. Any news on Sean?"

"Yes! He's been found, and he's okay."

"That's wonderful." Stella straightened, surged forward, and hugged Maggie tight. "I was thinking the worst."

"We all were." Maggie rubbed the younger woman's back. "Even if we didn't say it."

"Who found him?" Stella asked as Maggie stepped back.

"Frank, Elizabeth, and Caleb. They're on their way back."

"Do the other men know? Joshua will be so relieved."

Her chest swelling with a deep breath, Maggie waved

towards the area. "Frank sent up the flares as soon as he could. They'll all be back shortly."

"I'd best freshen up and come back. I don't want to miss this." Stella ran a hand over her dishevelled hair. Her eyes had brightened, but she still looked tired.

It was hard being heavily pregnant in this heat. Maggie remembered the lethargy, even though many years had passed since she'd carried her own babies. "Unless you need more rest."

Perking up, Stella redid her ponytail. "I'll be fine."

"Well, take it easy. I can wait if you like."

"Thanks, but I'll be fine."

Right. Maggie grimaced. She was being overly protective. "Sorry. I want to meet our new grandchild, but not tonight."

"I'm sure that won't happen." Stella patted her belly. "Everyone keeps telling me first babies are always late."

Maggie nodded. "My two were. But Emma's Sebastian came a week early, so there are always exceptions."

"I wouldn't mind being an exception."

"But not tonight."

"I guess not. Although it'd be kind of cool."

Maggie leaned on the railing and folded her arms. Dappled sunlight warmed her back. "The baby will come in God's timing, and when she arrives, your life will never be the same."

"Nap time might be a thing of the past?"

"So true. Enjoy it while you can."

"I will, but I'll take a quick shower now and head over. I want to be there when they all arrive."

"See you there. But take your time." Maggie squeezed her hand and left.

As she hurried back to the homestead, she prayed for the safe arrival of this new little grandchild. Grinning, she pictured Joshua holding the tiny bundle. Three years ago, that scenario seemed implausible, but following Julian's death, God transformed Joshua's life. Now he was a changed man.

Proof that God could indeed turn hearts of stone to hearts of flesh.

CHAPTER 11

*T*he last few hours played over in Sean's mind as Frank drove the quad back to the homestead. He'd come so close to being a goner. After his horse threw him and galloped away without him, he'd sat and contemplated his life.

It seemed God had thwarted his plan to ride off and not return.

Maybe God *had* listened, and this was His answer.

Stay and propose to Elizabeth. Stop running.

But then his foot got wedged between those rocks, the storm hit, and the water level rose. For hours, he'd expected to drown.

Those hours were the worst of his life. Unable to move the rocks on his own, he promised God that, if He saved him, he'd stop listening to the voices in his head and listen to Him instead.

And he'd propose to Elizabeth.

Just when he thought the end had come, Caleb appeared.

And then Uncle Frank and Elizabeth. He'd feared they were mirages. They weren't there—he was imagining them. Hallucinating.

But they were real. And they saved him.

He was alive.

His vision blurred.

He looked at Uncle Frank. So solid. A man to emulate.

Could Sean ever be like him?

For I know the plans I have for you. Plans to give you a future and a hope...

Elizabeth had shared that verse with him early on in their relationship. She knew he suffered from self-doubt, and she'd reminded him God loved him enough to send His only Son to earth not only to die for his sins but also to give him a life filled with peace and purpose.

Why had he resisted so long? He'd given his life to the Lord, but he hadn't been living the way God wanted him to. Clinging to self-doubt, he'd been afraid to commit for fear of failure.

But now, after coming so close to dying, he'd grasp life with both hands.

And he'd propose to Elizabeth.

What a fool he'd been. He'd almost lost everything, including his life, because of fear.

He reached up and covered her hand with his. Squeezed it.

And then he faced Uncle Frank. "Will you stop the quad?"

His uncle frowned. "Sure. Are you okay?"

Better than ever. His chest swelling, Sean nodded. "I need to do something."

He swivelled around in his seat, wincing when his ankle twisted. Then he took Elizabeth's hands in his.

Her brows lifted.

"This isn't the best place to do this, nor the most romantic, but I've been a fool, Liz. I don't know what I was running from, but I don't want to run anymore. Coming so close to drowning made me see things more clearly. Elizabeth Martin, I love you, and I want to spend the rest of my life with you. Will you do me the greatest honour and marry me?"

Her eyes widened. And then she beamed. "Of course, I'll marry you, you silly fool!" She stood and flung her arms around him and then lowered her face until their lips met. Her kiss, warm and sweet, was a balm to his wounded body and soul.

"I love you, Sean, and I can't wait to marry you."

"Nor me, you." He returned her kiss until Uncle Frank cleared his throat.

"Sorry to interrupt you lovebirds, but we need to keep going."

His mouth quirking, Sean released his fiancée and faced Uncle Frank. "Sorry."

"It's okay, son. I gather congratulations are in order."

"They are." Sean couldn't stop his grin from spreading as Elizabeth wrapped her arms around his neck from behind. "We're getting married."

"At last!" Uncle Frank slapped him on the thigh. "Congratulations, both of you. Maggie will be pleased. But now, we must push on." He restarted the quad, and it surged forward. Caleb was waiting on his bike around the next bend, and when they pulled alongside, relief filled his face. "I was about to come looking for you."

"No need. We just stopped for a moment."

"Right." He cocked his head, eyeing them, then shrugged, revved the bike, and took off.

Once, not long ago, perhaps even that morning, that motorbike sound would've triggered a desire within Sean to ride as fast as he could. To test the limits. But something had changed.

And he knew what it was. He was loved, and he no longer needed to prove himself.

Thank You, Lord. I'm so sorry it took me so long, but I'm grateful You saved me, grateful You're giving me this second chance. I promise I won't squander it. Thank You for Your love and thank You for Liz. Help me to be a good husband to her.

Back at the homestead, everyone, including Grandma Mary, gathered around and gushed when he and Elizabeth announced their engagement.

He'd almost ruined Christmas, but they'd forgiven him. Who would have thought an engagement announcement would have garnered this much excitement?

Adrenaline kept him going. But, when everyone began to disperse to prepare for dinner, the day caught up with him, and he flaked. He squeezed Elizabeth's hand. "I need to go inside for a bit. Have a shower, get out of these clothes."

"You'll need to use your gran's shower chair."

Shower chair? No way. "I'll be fine. I can stand." He tried to push to his feet. But his left leg gave way, and he collapsed back onto the chair. Great.

He met Liz's amused gaze. "Don't say a word."

"I won't."

He tried again and, this time, managed to stay upright. "See, I can do it."

"Okay, smartypants. Walk to the house."

"You don't think I can."

"Guess we'll see." She folded her arms and smirked.

He'd show her. He stepped out with his left foot, but as he transferred his weight to it, he winced. Words he didn't say anymore were on the tip of his tongue. He forged on. Didn't say them. Took another step. And then he gave in. "All right. You can help me walk. But I'm not using Gran's shower chair. I'll take a bath."

"Good, but you'll need help with that. I'll grab Joshua." She looked around and motioned for his cousin to join them.

Great. That's all he needed. So much for his macho cowboy image.

Joshua squeezed Stella's shoulder, loped over, and slapped Sean on the back. "Hey, mate. What's up?"

The words wouldn't come. He was a man. A cowboy. Cowboys didn't need help getting into a bath.

Elizabeth angled her head. Quirked her brow and gave him one of her looks. The one that told him he needed to man up.

He jutted his jaw. Cleared his throat, spoke low. "I need help to get in the bath."

He narrowed his eyes. Was his cousin smirking?

Maybe not.

Joshua shrugged. "No problem. I can help with that."

"Thanks." Sean gave a half smile.

Elizabeth rubbed his back. "I'll dress your ankle once you're out. I'm going to grab a quick shower and get out of these clothes."

He looked at them properly for the first time since he'd been rescued. She was still in her uniform.

ELIZABETH FOLLOWED Sean and Joshua into the house. His cabin didn't have a bath, and with the house closer, it made sense for him to freshen up there. Plus, her medical bag was in her room next to Mrs. Mary's.

David said he'd grab fresh clothes for Sean. With all the men needing showers, she wanted to get in first in case they ran out of hot water. Was that selfish? After tumbling around in those rapids, she needed a hot shower. If Sean hadn't been using the bath, she might have been tempted to have one herself.

Sean was limping and leaning on Joshua, but the sight of him gave her heart palpitations. The man she loved had proposed, and they were engaged! She could never have imagined the circumstances. What a story they'd have to tell their children and grandchildren.

Her heart warmed further. Only yesterday, she was thinking she might never have a family, but now, hope buoyed her. Sean would be a great dad, even if he didn't think so. Their kids would have so much fun.

But where would they live?

At Goddard Downs? In Sean's man cave?

Eek.

It'd need a lot of sprucing.

And she'd have to give up nursing.

She inhaled deeply. Why was she worrying about all these things? Hadn't she gotten what she wanted? The man she loved... Everything else would fall into place.

Thank You, Lord. Forgive me for thinking too far ahead and worrying needlessly.

Joshua and Sean peeled off into the main bathroom while she continued to the guest bathroom, stopping by her room to grab a change of clothes.

Although a shorts girl who rarely wore dresses, she'd packed one, just in case. Celebrating Christmas and an engagement had to warrant wearing it. Lifting the flowing summer frock out of the case, she hugged it to her body and grinned. Sean would be surprised.

The shower was bliss, but she didn't hog the hot water and turned it to cool after a few minutes. Refreshed, she stepped out and dried herself before slipping on the frock.

Before even doing her hair and make-up, she felt different. More feminine. Maybe she should wear dresses more often.

Five minutes later, she emerged from the bathroom and grabbed her medical bag.

Sean and Joshua were walking down the hallway. Sean was wearing khaki shorts and a short-sleeved white button-up shirt. His eyes widened, and he did a one-handed wolf-whistle.

With her cheeks warming, she tucked a strand of hair behind her ear. Wow. Did a dress make that much difference?

"What's with the dress?"

Her fingers fiddled with the skirt. "Thought the occasion warranted it."

His eyes sparkled. "You should wear them more often."

"Maybe I will." She swished side to side, enjoying the feel of it. Then her gaze dropped to his ankle. "How is it?"

"I'll live."

"I'm glad. Let's go to the living room, and I'll dress it."

Joshua stepped aside. "I'll leave you to it. I should check on Stella."

Her head jerked up, the nurse in her snapping to attention. "Is she all right?"

"I think so, although she doesn't seem quite herself." Joshua kneaded the back of his neck.

"I'll check on her once I've done Sean's ankle."

"Thanks." He slapped her shoulder in passing. "I appreciate that."

As he strode off, she helped Sean into the living room, but as soon as they were inside, he pulled her close and pressed his lips to hers.

"Sean! What if somebody comes in?"

"Does it matter?"

"I guess not." She responded to his kisses until a voice interrupted them.

"I'm glad to see you two got together."

"Mrs Mary!" They separated, and Elizabeth wrapped her arms around her body. "I didn't know you were in here."

"Obviously. But it doesn't matter. Seems there was no need for me to speak to my grandson after all."

His arm still around Elizabeth's waist, he frowned at his gran. "What do you mean, Gran?"

"I was going to tell you to stop dillydallying around and propose to this girl before you lost her, but you beat me to it. Congratulations." She held out her hands. "I can't tell you how pleased I am for you."

Sean stepped forward and took her hands. "I was stupid, wasn't I?"

"Perhaps. Scared might be a better word."

"You're right. Getting married still scares the crap out of me, but nearly drowning made me realise how much I love Liz and how I didn't want to live my life without her." He looked behind and met her gaze.

Swallowing the lump in her throat, she placed her hand on his shoulder.

Tenderness softened Mrs. Mary's gaze. "God will bless and guide you. Put Him first in your marriage, and you won't go wrong."

"Thanks, Gran. We'll do that, won't we, Liz?"

Heat prickled Elizabeth's eyes. How blessed they were. God had saved Sean in more ways than one. "Absolutely. Now, I need to dress Sean's ankle, and while I'm here, I'll check your wounds as well."

"No need, dear. Olivia did a good job. They're fine."

"Okay. But you'll let me know if they're bothering you, won't you?"

"They won't."

Elizabeth bit her lip. No doubting where Sean got his doggedness.

She attended to his ankle and secured a bandage around it. The bruising would deepen over the next days, and she'd need to keep an eye on the wound. As with Mrs. Mary's wounds, infection could set in at any time, especially in the humid weather.

She straightened and repacked her bag. Mrs. Mary was starting to doze, her head bobbing. Elizabeth went over and touched her shoulder. "Are you coming out for dinner?"

Mrs. Mary blinked. "Of course. I wouldn't miss it for the world." She went to stand but struggled to get out of her chair.

Elizabeth helped her up and placed her walking stick in her hand. "I wish you'd use your walker."

"Bah!" She waved Elizabeth off. "I don't need it."

"Okay…"

Sean chuckled as he got to his feet.

"Don't laugh, sonny boy. This will be you one day."

An image of growing old with Sean flashed through Elizabeth's mind. A crazy thought, but it warmed her, nevertheless.

They headed out of the room and down the hallway. Passing the kitchen, Elizabeth paused and asked Janella if she needed any help.

"Thanks, but it's all in hand. Wade's been a great help." Love shone in Janella's eyes as she gazed up at the man.

Seemed love was in the air, as well as cinnamon and spice.

CHAPTER 12

*M*aggie hummed to the Christmas song coming from the speakers on the exterior of the house as she placed salads on the serving table. With the Christmas Eve festivities underway, the joy of the season filled not only the air but also her being.

God was so good. Sean was safe, and he and Elizabeth were engaged, along with Janella and Wade, although no one else knew.

What a special Christmas. One to remember.

Joshua and David stood at the barbecue, chatting and laughing while cooking the meat, but where was Frank? He'd been with them moments ago.

Ah. There he was. Greeting some guests who'd just arrived. He was so in his element, and seeing him so happy and relaxed warmed her heart. She wandered over to join him. She'd never thought she'd be a pastor's wife, but she enjoyed supporting

Frank in his ministry. Linking her arm through his, she smiled at the family that had just arrived.

The woman was Indigenous and stood behind her husband as she gazed around. Maggie let go of Frank, stepped towards her, and extended her hand. "Hello, I'm Maggie. Welcome to Goddard Downs."

The woman hesitated, but when she took Maggie's hand and smiled, her teeth glistened against her dark skin. "I'm Norma. Thanks for inviting us."

"You're very welcome. And who are these two?" Crouching, Maggie smiled at the two curly-haired youngsters hiding behind their mother's legs. They looked at her with large round eyes.

Norma peeled their hands off her legs and held them. "Come on. Tell the lady your names."

"Lucy," the little girl on her right said.

After another prompt from her mother, the smaller of the two announced she was Wanda.

"They're lovely names. Would you like to come with me and meet the other children?" Maggie held her hands out to them.

"Go on. The lady won't bite." Norma nudged them, and they took Maggie's hands.

"They'll be fine. Don't worry about them."

Norma gave a nod before Maggie crossed the grassed area with the little girls alongside her. They weren't twins, but they were close in age. "How old are you, Lucy?"

"Four. And Wanda's three."

"And are you excited about Christmas?"

"Mummy said that, if we're good, Santa might come."

"And have you been good?"

"Sometimes I do naughty things."

Maggie chuckled. "So long as you're sorry, I'm sure Santa will still come."

"I hope so." The little girl's round face brightened. "Mummy said Santa might bring me a bike."

"That would be exciting. And what about you, Wanda? What would you like Santa to bring you for Christmas?" Maggie had to bite her tongue. She didn't like talking about Santa like this, but it wasn't her place to enlighten the little girls.

Wanda shrugged. "I don't know."

"I'm sure he'll bring you something nice, anyway." They reached the other children who were playing a game of tag on the open paddock.

Maggie waved to Isobel. "Hey, Issie. Could you come here a minute, please?"

Isobel looked around and then sprinted in their direction. Her face was red, and she was panting.

"Sorry to interrupt, but these two little girls would like to join in. Is that okay?"

Isobel nodded. "Sure."

Maggie introduced the girls. When they hesitated to go with Issie, Maggie assured them she'd stay and watch.

As they scrambled off with Isobel, Maggie shielded her eyes from the setting sun. The air had become more bearable, though the humidity still clung to her pores. The storm had come and gone quickly today, but she hated to think how Sean must have felt as the water level rose in that creek.

Such a miracle he'd been found. No doubt God had led

Frank there, just like He'd led the three wise men to Bethlehem all those years ago. How God actually spoke remained a mystery, but He sure did. He might not speak in an audible voice, but His leading was there for those prepared to listen.

Her gaze shifted to the laughing children. What lay ahead for each of them? The world was changing. With so much strife everywhere, people seemed more anxious. Here on the station, one could put on blinders and not think about what was happening out there, but one day, these children would leave Goddard Downs and be exposed to life outside its safe walls.

How she'd love to protect them all. To ensure they never knew a moment of strife, but that was impossible. And unreasonable. They'd go out and forge their way, just as Caleb and Sasha were.

The siblings had changed since moving to Darwin. They were maturing into wonderful young adults who loved the Lord, and she was so proud of them, especially with everything they'd been through.

Frank had told her how Caleb had stepped up and faced his fears today. It would have been so easy for him not to venture into that water, but he had. And he saved Sean's life.

Although her grandmother's heart cared about each of the children, there was no need to worry. Entrusting them to her heavenly Father was the best thing she could do because He loved them even more than she did.

Lord, I entrust these precious children to You. May they seek You with all their hearts, and may they know the breadth and depth of Your love so they can withstand the temptations and challenges ahead of them. May they grow in Your love and become salt and light in this world. Father, bless each and every one of them, I pray. In Jesus' precious name. Amen.

Footsteps sounded in the long grass. Then Serena slipped her arm around her waist. "A penny for your thoughts."

"Oh, luv, I was just wondering what the future holds for all these kids."

"Mum! You're sounding morose. It's Christmas!"

"I know. It's been a crazy day, though."

"It has." Serena pressed her cheek to Maggie's. "But everything's fine. You worry too much."

"I do not."

Drawing back, Serena lifted a brow. "Really?"

"Really. Okay. Maybe a tad."

"Mm. Anyway, dinner's ready, and I came to get you and the kids."

"That won't be easy. They're having a lot of fun."

"Tell them there's ice cream, and they'll come."

Chuckling, Maggie waved to them. "Dinner's ready, guys. You need to come back."

They gave a collective groan until Serena shouted, "Ice cream for dessert!" Then it was a race to see who could get there first.

Of course, the big boys won, but Oliver came a close third.

Serena caught them up and gathered them in while Frank welcomed everyone.

In knee-length cargo shorts, a Christmassy button-up short-sleeved shirt, and brown loafers, he looked so relaxed. And handsome. Maggie could gaze at him all day.

He smiled as he surveyed the crowd. "Welcome, everyone. It's such a blessing to share this Christmas Eve supper with you all. Let's give thanks to our heavenly Father, and then please help yourselves to this amazing spread. Let's pray."

As he bowed his head, Maggie placed her hands on the two little girls' shoulders. They'd fitted right in and seemed happy enough to be with Isobel, taken under her sisterly care.

"Heavenly Father, we pause at this special time, the night before Your Son's birthday, to give thanks for the many blessings You've bestowed on us. Even today, we've seen Your mighty hand at work in our lives. We give thanks for Sean's safe return and for his and Elizabeth's engagement. Bless their relationship, Lord, and may they grow deeper in love with each other and with You.

"Lord, we also give thanks for this food and for the hands that prepared it. We feel blessed to have Janella and the children back in the fold, even if it's not for long. But mostly, we give thanks for the amazing sacrifice You made when you sent Jesus to earth as a baby to rescue mankind from sin and death. For that gift, we are eternally grateful. In Jesus' precious name. Amen."

After a collective amen, Frank reminded everyone about the service starting at eight p.m. before inviting their guests to serve themselves from the table ahead of the family. Other neighbours had arrived—some Maggie knew, some she didn't.

She took the little girls by the hand and returned them to Norma, who was standing in line at the food table with her husband.

Norma gave a grateful smile. "Thanks for looking after them."

"You're more than welcome. They had a great time."

"It looks that way. They enjoy playing with other children."

"You'll have to come over more often. I'm thinking of starting a weekly group for young mothers in the new year." Maggie blinked. Where had that come from? That was the first she knew of it.

Norma's eyes lit up. "A playgroup?"

"Ah, yes. Something like that." Maggie's mind whirled. Not just a playgroup. A support group for mothers who often felt isolated and alone. She'd started this journey researching that article about how women on remote cattle stations managed with little contact with other women. Here at Goddard Downs, the women had each other, but on many of the smaller stations, they didn't have that support. This was what God was calling her to. She felt certain of it. Amazing. And it felt right. Since returning from her and Frank's trip, she'd been seeking God's will for her life. Gardening, painting, and penning the occasional article were all well and good, but something had been missing. Could this be it?

Norma beamed. "That sounds awesome. Please let me know when it'll be."

Almost in shock, Maggie nodded. "Absolutely."

She left the family and joined Frank. He'd stepped away from the crowd and was gazing across the paddock at the darkening sky while sipping a drink.

He slipped his arm across her shoulders and kissed the side of her head. "Hey, darling."

She leaned into him. "Hey, yourself. It's gorgeous, isn't it?"

"It sure is. God certainly knows how to paint a picture."

"He certainly does."

CHAPTER 13

Seated on a rug under a starlit sky, Elizabeth snuggled against Sean while waiting for the Christmas Eve service to begin. Mrs. Mary was in a chair beside them, a rug over her knees despite the balmy evening.

A temporary stage had been erected, and everyone quietened when the Christmas carol that had been playing stopped and a voice—Sasha's?—came over the loudspeaker.

"'So Joseph also went up from the town of Nazareth in Galilee to Judea, to Bethlehem the town of David, because he belonged to the house and line of David. He went there to register with Mary, who was pledged to be married to him and was expecting a child. While they were there, the time came for the baby to be born, and she gave birth to her firstborn, a son. She wrapped him in cloths and placed him in a manger, because there was no guest room available for them.'"

Lights flashed on, revealing an entire nativity scene,

complete with a donkey and a sheep, as well as Mary, Joseph, and baby Jesus in a manger.

The voice continued, and the scene changed to a group of shepherds tending their flock.

"'And there were shepherds living out in the fields nearby, keeping watch over their flocks at night. An angel of the Lord appeared to them, and the glory of the Lord shone around them, and they were terrified. But the angel said to them, "Do not be afraid. I bring you good news that will cause great joy for all the people. Today in the town of David a Saviour has been born to you; He is the Messiah, the Lord. This will be a sign to you: You will find a baby wrapped in cloths and lying in a manger."

"'Suddenly a great company of the heavenly host appeared with the angel, praising God and saying, "Glory to God in the highest heaven, and on earth peace to those on whom his favour rests."'

"'When the angels had left them and gone into heaven, the shepherds said to one another, "Let's go to Bethlehem and see this thing that has happened, which the Lord has told us about."'"

The scene changed again.

"'The shepherds, finding the newborn baby Jesus, worshipped Him, and glorified and praised God for all the things they had heard and seen, which were just as they had been told.'"

The lights dimmed and then shone on Frank, who was beaming. "Wasn't that amazing? The kids did a wonderful job, didn't they? Let's show our thanks." He clapped, and everyone else joined in as the children, along with Serena, the director and instigator, whom Frank had waved up, stood on the stage and bowed.

After the applause, the stage was cleared, and Frank invited Caleb and Sasha to join him. He placed his hands on their shoulders. "I'm proud to announce that these two are leading the singing tonight. Caleb and Sasha, the stage is yours."

Sasha sat at the keyboard while Caleb stepped closer to the microphone. "Hey, everyone. Would you please stand and join us in singing 'Silent Night'?"

As everyone stood, Elizabeth told Mrs. Mary there was no need for her to stand.

"But I want to, dear."

Of course, she did. Her chest warming, Elizabeth helped her up and supported her as the carol began, her heart swelling with joy as she sang.

"Silent night, holy night!
All is calm, all is bright.
Round yon Virgin, Mother and Child.
Holy infant so tender and mild,
Sleep in heavenly peace,
Sleep in heavenly peace.
Silent night, holy night!
Shepherds quake at the sight.
Glories stream from heaven afar
Heavenly hosts sing Alleluia,
Christ the Saviour is born!
Christ the Saviour is born."

After the round of carols, Isobel read from Matthew chapter 1, and then Frank gave a short message.

Once he finished, he invited everyone to light their candles and wave them as the stage lights dimmed, and they sang the final carol, "Away in a Manger".

The evening finished with each of the children receiving a gift.

As Elizabeth helped Mrs. Mary to her feet, Stella waddled towards her, holding her stomach and grinning.

Joshua was with her, but his eyes were wide. "Liz." His voice broke, coming out high-pitched. "Stella's waters just broke. What do we do?"

"It's okay, Josh." Elizabeth rubbed his arm, trying to calm him. "I'll take Stella inside and do a quick check."

Mrs. Mary patted her hand. "Don't worry about me, dear. Sean can look after me."

Hmm. How would that work since neither could walk without assistance? But maybe they could hold each other up. And maybe it'd do Sean good to spend time with his gran. "Ask for help if you need it."

Sean jostled her into a quick hug and kissed her cheek. "We'll be fine."

As their gazes met, gratitude and love for this man she'd almost lost warmed her. She softened her voice. "I love you."

His eyes sparkling, he pressed a finger to her nose. "Not as much as I love you."

Joshua cleared his throat.

They both chuckled before Elizabeth turned her attention to Stella. "Sorry. Are you sure it was your waters?"

Stella nodded. "It was like a flood."

"Let's get you inside."

"I said I wanted the baby to come sooner, but I didn't expect her to come tonight."

"Babies come in God's timing, so He must have thought Christmas was the perfect time for your little one to make an appearance."

Stella beamed. "It'll sure be special. Will I need to go to the hospital?"

"Probably, but let's examine you first."

Elizabeth walked with the couple to the homestead, although Joshua carried Stella most of the way, despite Elizabeth assuring him there was no need.

She settled Stella onto Elizabeth's bed and performed an examination. "Well, I can confirm that your waters have indeed broken."

"I told you."

"I know you did. We just needed to be sure."

Stella swung her feet to the floor and straightened her clothing. "Should I go to the hospital?"

"Not yet. Let's wait for your contractions to begin."

"And that could take forever, hey?"

After Elizabeth removed her gloves and placed them in a bin, Stella grabbed her wrist. "If it happens quickly, you can deliver it, right?"

With a gulp, Elizabeth braved a tentative yes. She'd much rather Stella delivered her baby in the hospital, but she *had* delivered babies before. As part of her training in midwifery, she'd been assigned to an Indigenous community where the women gave birth in the open. Most of the babies she'd helped deliver had survived. The one loss haunted her. She didn't want another. "I'm thinking you'll be able to enjoy Christmas day tomorrow and then we'll head into the hospital, but whatever happens, I'll be here for you."

Stella's face softened. "Thanks. I don't know what I'd do without you."

As Elizabeth smiled, she prayed for wisdom, because something inside her was telling her she'd need it.

CHAPTER 14

*A*fter settling his grandmother into bed, Sean hobbled outside onto the verandah for some fresh air. The crowd had dispersed, and everything had been packed away. Only the Christmas lights twinkling in the trees hinted it was Christmas Eve.

As he eased onto a cane rocker and rubbed his thighs, a dull ache in his ankle reminded him of his ordeal. What an idiot he'd been. He could have died.

God, I'm sorry I'm such a blockhead. I wouldn't have blamed You if You'd given up on me, but thank You that You didn't. I can't believe Liz agreed to marry me. I don't know how to be a good husband, but I want to learn. Teach me Your ways, Lord. Help me to trust You and not to listen to the voices telling me I'm useless.

He exhaled low and deep. *I've got a long way to go, but I won't squander this second chance You've given me. Help me to grow into the man You want me to be, Lord.*

A hand touched his shoulder. Liz? He reached up.

Nothing.

He looked around. No one was there.

A tingle ran through him.

Could God have placed His hand on him?

No way!

But as heat burned his eyes and his heart pounded, he sensed God's presence. The creator of the universe was with him.

Yea, I have loved thee with an everlasting love: therefore with loving kindness have I drawn thee.

Tears spilled down his cheeks, splashed his thighs. Such love he didn't deserve, but God had showered it on him anyway. He fell to his knees and wept.

Sometime later, another hand settled on his shoulder. A woman's. He lifted his gaze and looked into Liz's soft eyes.

She knelt beside him and cradled him in her arms. Rocked him like a baby. Pressed her lips to his head.

He breathed in her scent. Soaked up her warmth. Imbibed her essence.

She turned his face to hers and wiped his tears. Looked deep into his eyes. "Don't ever doubt my love, Sean. From the moment we met, I knew you were the man I wanted to spend my life with. It just took a while for you to catch up."

She wasn't wrong. Straightening, he palmed her cheeks. "I'm sorry, Liz. I've been such a dunderhead. I don't know what you see in me, but I give you my word that I'm going to be the best husband I can be."

"I believe you. I believe *in* you."

Heart crumpling, he pulled her to himself. Ran his lips over her hair. Found her mouth. Kissed her like he'd not kissed her before. Passion ran through him. "Let's not wait long to get married."

"Let's not."

She kissed him back, but he pulled away, needing to stop before passion carried him places he shouldn't go. He stroked her cheek. "I don't want to go inside. Let's do something crazy tonight."

Her eyes sparkled. "Like what?"

"I don't know. Climb a mountain. Watch the sunrise. What do you think?"

"For a start, you can't climb a mountain."

His gaze dropped to his ankle. "Oh yeah. I forgot. But we could ride."

"We could. But Stella could go into labour at any time."

"What if we stay here?"

"On the verandah?"

He nodded. "What's wrong with that?"

"It's uncomfortable."

"You win. Let's go inside and have hot chocolate."

She smiled. "That sounds better. But unless Stella's in labour, we can get up early, and I'll drive us to the ridge. We can have breakfast and be back before anyone knows we're gone."

"Won't the kids be up early?"

"Probably. But I can sneak out the back way."

"It's a deal."

"Great. And, Sean"—she held his gaze—"I don't want to wait long to get married. We've waited too long already."

Closing his eyes, he pressed his forehead to hers. "That was my fault."

"It doesn't matter." Her breath feathered over his face. "Let's look forward, not backward."

Sounded good. He shifted his weight to push to his feet. Winced. Stupid ankle. But God had made good his foolish actions. If his horse hadn't thrown him and he hadn't become stuck in that creek, he might never have proposed. And he could have been miles from Goddard Downs, perhaps never to return. God had indeed turned his foolish actions around.

Liz held out her hand. "Let me help."

With gratitude and humility, he took the hand of the woman he loved.

Once on his feet, he slipped his arm around her waist and tugged her close. "How I love you, Elizabeth Martin."

"And how I love you, Sean Goddard."

WHILE SIPPING HOT CHOCOLATE, Elizabeth listened to the chatter in the room. Although it was well past her normal bedtime, Mrs. Mary hadn't stayed in bed and was now seated beside Elizabeth on the living room couch. Sean sat on the floor at their feet, and now and then, Elizabeth leaned forward and twiddled his dark hair, barely able to believe they were engaged.

Despite their excitement, the younger children were all asleep in the back room. Their parents had told them they needed to go to bed so Santa would come the following morning. Elizabeth wondered at that, but there was no harm in it. The kids knew Christmas was about the birth of Jesus, so a little make-believe was okay.

Maggie was organising a game of Christmas Who Am I? and handing out Post-it Notes with the name of a famous Christmas character written on each. "Okay, turn to the person on your right and stick your Post-it Note to their forehead."

Elizabeth faced Mrs. Mary. "Do you want to play?"

"Of course. I wouldn't miss it for the world. Stick it to me."

"There you go, then." With gentle fingers, Elizabeth pressed the lime-green paper to Mrs. Mary's forehead. She'd never guess who she was. But then, Elizabeth mightn't guess hers either. The characters could be from the first Christmas when Jesus was born or any popular Christmas movie, past or present. Hmm.

Sean then stuck a pink piece to her forehead. He already wore a blue one. Ebenezer Scrooge. Would Sean even have heard of him?

It could be an interesting game.

Maggie stood in the doorway. "Okay, who wants to go first?"

From his armchair where he sat with his legs crossed, Frank raised his hand. "I will, luv."

The look that passed between them warmed Elizabeth's heart. If she and Sean could love each other as much as Frank and Maggie did at their age, she'd be stoked. Her parents divorced when she was young. Until she met the Goddard family when Stella and Joshua got together, Elizabeth hadn't seen many happy marriages, so their love gave her hope.

She squeezed Sean's hand and prayed silently for God's blessing on them.

And so, the game began. It took Frank six questions to

guess his character—Kevin McCallister from the movie *Home Alone*. Mrs. Mary got hers in two—George Bailey from the movie *It's a Wonderful Life*. How did she do that? Elizabeth had no idea. Hers was much harder, and she almost gave up. But, when she asked if her character was an animal, she guessed that she was the donkey that carried Mary to Bethlehem.

The game finished, and as everyone was saying how much they enjoyed it but that they really should go to bed, Janella and Wade stood with their arms around each other. Janella tucked a strand of wavy dark hair behind her ear and cleared her voice. "Hey, everyone, we have an announcement."

The room quietened, and all turned to them.

Janella lifted her gaze to Wade, and after his nod, she looked at Elizabeth. "We didn't want to steal yours and Sean's limelight, but we couldn't keep it a secret any longer." Beaming, she leaned into Wade. "Wade and I are engaged!"

Cheers filled the room, and everyone, apart from Mrs. Mary, rose and hugged the couple. When the noise lessened, Frank dinged his glass. "We should pray for both of these couples. What a special occasion. Janella and Wade, on behalf of everyone here, I want to convey our congratulations and wish you all of God's blessings. You, too, Sean and Elizabeth. We're thrilled for all of you, and I'd love to pray for you."

Smiling, he bowed his head. "Lord God, what a wonderful Christmas blessing. To have not one, but two engagements is truly awesome. Bless these special couples. May they look to You always, and may they grow in love for You and for each other. Bless them now, I pray. Oh, and we also want to bring before You Stella, Joshua, and the new member of their family who's on her way. Bless them all at this special time, and may

You grant Stella a safe delivery. We can't wait to meet the new baby. In Jesus' precious name. Amen."

When Sean slipped his arm across Elizabeth's shoulders, she snuggled close. She would never forget this day, with all its twists and turns and blessings and challenges.

Her gaze swung to Stella. Would the night bring yet another twist?

CHAPTER 15

S ometime during the night, Elizabeth woke to her phone buzzing. With a sense of foreboding, she reached for it. Joshua's name flashed on the screen.

"Josh. What's happened?" She answered in a whispered voice as Mrs. Mary was in the next room and, in the still of the night, sound carried.

"Stella's having contractions." Joshua sounded breathless.

Elizabeth sat up. "How far apart?"

"Continual."

"Hang tight. I'll be right there." The contractions wouldn't be continual, but no need to tell him that. With Stella in pain, he was worried.

"Thanks. I don't know what to do." Yep. Panic screeched in his voice.

"Stay calm. Rub her back. Hold her hand. Pray."

"I'll do my best."

"Good. She'll be fine."

Elizabeth swung her legs onto the floor and turned on her bedside lamp. She'd expected this. Although there'd been no indication Stella would start labour during the night, Elizabeth sensed she would and prepared. Her medical bag was packed, but if time allowed, she'd get Stella to the hospital in Kununurra rather than delivering the baby herself.

Somehow, though, she sensed time wasn't on their side.

Lord, please go with me and grant me wisdom. Be with Stella and her unborn baby. Grant her a safe delivery. In Jesus' name. Amen.

She dressed, grabbed her bag, keys, and phone, then turned off the light, and tiptoed out of her room and down the hall.

The floorboards squeaked. Great. She paused outside Mrs. Mary's room. The dear lady was snoring, but Elizabeth needed to tell someone she wasn't there in case she woke. Frank and Maggie were in their cottage, and Janella would be tired after the long drive from Darwin. It had to be Olivia.

Outside, Elizabeth pulled out her phone and sent her a text.

Elizabeth: *Sorry to wake you! Stella's in labour, and I'm off to check on her. I'll keep you posted. Can you please listen out for your gran?*

She didn't expect an immediate answer, but she got one.

Olivia: *Wow! Yes, I'll listen out. Let me know if I can do anything. I'll be praying. xx*

Elizabeth: *Thank you xx*

With that sorted, guided by the light shining through the trees, she hurried along the track towards Joshua and Stella's cabin, her thoughts turning to those other lights two thousand years ago that guided shepherds to the most important birth of all time. The birth of Jesus, the Son of God.

While the birth of Stella's baby could never be compared

with the birth of Jesus, it would still make this Christmas Day one she'd never forget.

On her right, light from another cabin shone through the trees. Her eyes narrowed. Sean's cabin? Was he awake?

Her heartbeat kicked up a notch.

Could she detour? It would only add a minute. No. She had to get to Stella.

She pushed on, but in her haste, she tripped on a tree root and landed flat on her face. Great. Blowing out a breath, she scrambled to her feet and brushed the dirt off her clothes and body. She must look a treat, but never mind. She hadn't broken anything.

She reached the cabin and hurried up the steps.

Joshua let her in, his face white.

She patted his arm in passing. "Women have given birth from the beginning of time. Stella will be fine."

He nodded but didn't look convinced.

A bloodcurdling scream came from the bedroom, and she hurried to her cousin. Hunched over, Stella gripped her stomach. Elizabeth bent down and rubbed her back. "Take a slow breath through your nose. Hold it. Blow out."

Stella did what she was told.

"That's it. Now, do it again. Breathe in. Hold. Blow out."

The contraction passed, and Stella straightened, her brow glistening with sweat. "I didn't know it was going to be this bad."

Elizabeth wiped Stella's brow with a handtowel. "Everybody says that." No doubt, she would too, when her time came. And then it hit her. She and Sean were engaged. Perhaps this time next year, *she* might be giving birth. Her lips lifted. But there was no time to dwell on that now.

She brushed damp hair away from her cousin's forehead. "Let me examine you. How far apart are your contractions?"

"About three minutes."

Right. Travelling to Kununurra was out of the question. The quick examination confirmed it.

"Is everything all right?" Joshua stood in the doorway. Poor guy, he looked so worried.

"Everything's fine. Your baby's on its way."

"Wow." He ran a hand across his hair.

"I need you to help me."

He stepped forward like an eager child. "What do you want me to do?"

"Fetch some towels."

"And hot water?"

"Sure." Anything to keep him busy.

The moment he left, another contraction hit.

"It's okay. Breathe in. Hold. Breathe out. Again." Elizabeth squeezed her cousin's hand and rubbed her back. "You're doing great."

The contraction passed. Joshua returned with towels and hot water.

"Thanks. Set the bowl on the floor and pass me the towels."

He followed her directions and helped slip a towel under Stella.

"What should I do now?"

"Sit beside her and hold her hand. Help her breathe through the contractions." She showed him how.

When the next contraction started, she encouraged them both. "You're doing great."

Now, she needed to get her act together—she had a baby to deliver. "Lord, please give me wisdom and clarity. Let this baby come into this world safely, I pray."

She pushed back memories of that delivery three years ago, the one that had gone horribly wrong. There was nothing more she could have done to save that baby. She didn't understand why God had allowed the tiny baby girl to die, but she had to trust in His goodness and sovereignty and rest in the fact that He could bring good out of something so sad.

But she wouldn't dwell on that loss. She'd do everything in her power to help Stella bring her baby into this world safely. If only there'd been time to go to the hospital. But there wasn't, and that's all there was to it.

She brushed her hands together and took a deep breath. "On the next contraction, I want you to start pushing."

Stella nodded. "Can you give me something for the pain?"

"I don't have anything—I'm sorry. But it'll be over soon. I promise."

And it was. Twenty minutes later, Stella delivered a healthy baby girl. Relief filled Elizabeth while she passed the tiny bundle to her mother. "She's gorgeous, and she's perfect."

Joshua sat beside Stella. Tears streamed down his cheeks when he touched his daughter's tiny pink fingers.

Elizabeth thought her heart would burst. *Thank You, Lord. Bless this baby girl. May she come to know and love You with all her heart.*

Stella beamed. "She shares Jesus' birthday. Such a blessing."

"It sure is."

Elizabeth left the new parents to enjoy time with their baby. Dawn was breaking, and through the trees, a figure strode towards her. Sean.

She ran down the steps and threw herself into his arms.

"Whoa. What's going on?" He held her at arms-length.

Her breaths came fast. "I was so scared something would go wrong, but Joshua and Stella have a beautiful baby girl."

"You did good."

"Not me. God and Stella."

"Don't underestimate yourself."

Chuckling, she batted at his chest. "Did you just hear what you said?"

He chuckled with her and snugged her to his side. "So, what about that breakfast?"

BACK IN THE MAIN HOUSE, news of Esther Rose Goddard's safe arrival travelled fast. Maggie received a text from Olivia at five a.m., and she and Frank dressed and drove the short distance to meet their newest granddaughter.

Joshua and Stella were seated on the lounge, cradling baby Esther, while all around, the family chattered and took turns admiring the tiny baby girl and congratulating the beaming couple.

Maggie stood in the doorway while Frank wove his way to his son and daughter-in-law. She could only imagine how he was feeling. Joshua had always been the wild son. The one he worried about the most, and yet, here he was, proud as punch as he cradled his baby daughter, whom he and Stella had named after Frank's beloved Esther.

Maggie's eyes brimmed when Joshua passed the tiny bundle to his father. The love on Frank's face was so evident. This little girl would be much loved. They were so very blessed.

Frank lifted his gaze and motioned for Maggie to join him. Sometimes she still felt like an outsider, but there was no need. Although little Esther wasn't her flesh and blood, she was her granddaughter, just as much as Oliver was Frank's grandson. They were family, and that's all that mattered.

Just as God had adopted each and every one of them as His special children, and they all were part of His family.

"She's gorgeous." Maggie squeezed Stella's hand. "You're very blessed."

Stella beamed. "We are. Elizabeth did an amazing job."

Maggie frowned. "Where is she?"

"Having breakfast with Sean out on the ridge."

"Oh. That's nice." She was so happy for them.

Olivia cleared her voice, and everyone, kids included, turned their attention to her. "Happy Christmas, everyone. And what a special one it is with the birth of this little baby on Jesus' birthday. We should start the day by giving thanks." She smiled at Frank. "Dad, would you do the honours?"

"I'd love to." He was still holding baby Esther, which was appropriate as he prayed a blessing over her. "Lord God, we give You all the thanks and praise for the safe arrival of Esther Rose Goddard. Bless her and keep her. Make Your face shine upon her and give her peace. And bless her parents. May they walk in Your ways and raise her in a home that puts You first. And, Lord, on this special morning, we give You thanks for the gift of Your Son, the Lord Jesus Christ, whom You sent to earth to save mankind. As we celebrate Jesus' birthday today, may we be mindful of Your great love and sacrifice, and may we grow in grace and in the knowledge of our Lord and Saviour, in whose name we pray. Amen."

A chorus of amens filled the room. Frank handed baby Esther back to Stella, and Olivia announced that breakfast would be served in the dining room before presents were opened.

The children all complained.

"Can't we open one each?" Isobel tugged on her mother's hand.

Olivia looked to Frank. Raised a brow.

"Oh, come on, Olivia." Frank laughed. "It's Christmas. Let the kids open their presents."

"Yes! Thank you, Grandpa." Isobel beamed at him across the room.

"You're welcome. So, who's going to be my helper today?"

All the younger children raised their hands and called out "Me!"

"Oh. That's a hard choice." Frank stroked his chin.

Maggie leaned closer to him. "I think you should choose Isobel since she instigated this."

"Good point." He faced the children. "Isobel, you can be my helper today."

The children seemed happy with that, especially as the presents were distributed and they forgot they hadn't been chosen.

Maggie and Frank had bought or made gifts for all the children. She'd spent hours online trying to find the perfect gift for each, but in the end, she and Frank had driven to Darwin and spent three days shopping. It turned into a mini holiday as they squeezed in a meal at Pearls, the restaurant Frank had taken her to on their first date, and they enjoyed the sunset over the bay after wandering through the Mindil markets where they bought many of their gifts. They also visited Janella, Caleb, and Sasha, Jeremy, Emma, and their children, and Frank's sister and brother-in-law, Bethany and Graham.

But as they drove back to Goddard Downs along that long, slow road, a deep realisation that Darwin was no longer her home enveloped Maggie. Goddard Downs had seeped into her soul and was now the place she called home. She loved the wide-open spaces. The beauty and ruggedness of The Kimberley. The rich colours, the history, the people.

She'd looked at Frank and smiled. And of course, she loved this handsome cowboy who'd captured her heart and inspired her every day to live her best life. Who knew how many years they had left on this earth, but she was determined to make the most of every single one.

And now, as the children squealed over their gifts, she gave thanks for each person she was blessed to call family.

A short while later, they adjourned to the dining room and enjoyed a buffet breakfast of waffles with blueberries and maple syrup, scrambled eggs and bacon, and platters of fresh summer fruit.

While they were eating, Sean and Elizabeth returned, looking so much in love that Maggie's heart warmed further, if that were possible.

There were so many things to be thankful for. A new baby. Two engagements. But most of all, the birth of Jesus.

After breakfast, everyone prepared for church. The service was being held in the open-air chapel Frank had built after returning from his and Maggie's trip. Even with seating for fifty, on most Sunday mornings, the seats filled quickly, and latecomers sat or stood around the edges. Today, as the band played Christmas hymns and people continued to arrive, some having driven more than two hours to get there, there'd be standing room only.

Olivia and Janella offered refreshments while people arrived, and everybody was filled with Christmas cheer.

As Frank led the service, peace filled Maggie's heart. She couldn't have asked for a better Christmas. Not only was Maggie surrounded by family and celebrating two engagements and a new baby, but Isobel had gotten her four baby chickens.

All was well in the world. She had peace with God, peace with others, and peace in her heart.

The following morning when she woke, Frank wasn't in bed, but banging came from outside. Pulling on a robe, she hurried onto the deck.

"Frank! What are you doing?"

He grinned. "Building you a carport. Merry Christmas."

The early morning sunlight cast a golden glow over his strong-boned face, accentuating the stubble on his firm jaw and deepening the blue of his eyes. Could she love him any more than she did now?

She bounced down the steps, threw her arms around his neck, and kissed him with gratefulness. "Thank you. This is the best Christmas gift ever."

EPILOGUE

*S*ean wanted to elope. Who wanted to bother with all that wedding hoo-ha? Not him. No way. But Elizabeth insisted the family would never forgive them. Even Josh had told him to man up, slapping him on the back, and telling him to do it for Liz.

At least, Liz had been happy to get hitched at Goddard Downs, and not some fancy place like El Questro. He couldn't have handled that.

But what did it matter? He was marrying Liz, the woman he loved.

So, here he was, dressed up like a stuffed chook in a tan three-piece suit, complete with a flower in a buttonhole. A flower? Really? He ran his hand under the collar and loosened the button at his neck as he studied his reflection in the full-length mirror in Uncle Frank's cottage.

It was all happening. He exhaled a long breath and tried to

calm the butterflies in his stomach. Josh had told him feeling anxious was normal, but far out he wished it was all over and he and Liz could ride off into the sunset and leave this craziness behind.

They should have eloped.

But that would have been the coward's way. And he was done with running away.

No, he had to do this. He'd stand before everyone and commit to love and cherish Liz for the rest of their lives. He owed her that.

And Uncle Frank said the ceremony was important because marriage was a sacred covenant, a holy relationship between a man and a woman, instituted by God. The vows he and Liz would share weren't just for each other. They would be inviting God into their marriage and making a public commitment before the Lord, their family, and their friends.

So yep, he was doing it.

He swallowed hard. Drew a long breath. Turned and faced Josh.

A twinkle lit his cousin's eye as he studied Sean while leaning against the doorframe.

"Well?" Sean angled his head. Narrowed his gaze.

"Well, you scrubbed up good." His cousin chuckled.

Sean shook his head. "Never again. Give me jeans and boots any day."

"I hear you. But you're doing it for Liz, and this is what she wants."

"So, we should get out of here." Sean strode for the door.

"Yep. You don't want to keep your bride waiting."

ELIZABETH STOOD in front of the mirror and studied the simple, yet elegant, wedding gown Sarah had made for her. Elizabeth didn't do fancy, but she wanted to look her best for Sean.

The delicate lace on the shoulder straps was perfect, and the soft chiffon gown flattered her figure. Her hair was curled and pinned up with cream silk flowers.

Stella stood behind her and squeezed her shoulders. "You look like a princess."

Elizabeth met her cousin's gaze in the mirror. "I can't believe it's happening."

"Are you okay?"

Was she? The past three months had been a whirlwind. Sean had wanted them to elope. Although tempted, she couldn't do that to the family.

But pulling off a wedding in such a short time frame had been a challenge. Plus, she'd wanted them to visit his parents to break the news of their engagement, but Sean insisted on telling them over Zoom. He wasn't making the trip to Perth.

She kind of understood. Perth was a long way, and they both needed to work, but still. He needed to clear the air between them.

His parents had arrived two days before the wedding. His mum was in a wheelchair. With her now partially blind and her MS progressing fast, Sean's dad had become her full-time carer.

When Elizabeth met them at Sarah's home in Kununurra,

the way Stephen looked after Miriam with such love left Elizabeth wondering what had made him so hard on Sean.

A man thing? Were they both as stubborn as each other?

And then, that first night when Sean came for dinner, he'd taken his father outside at her bidding. She didn't know what was said, but whatever it was, the air was cleared when they returned. What a relief.

Elizabeth inhaled as she nodded at Stella. "I'm okay. Although I'm wondering if we shouldn't have just eloped like Sean wanted to do."

Waving a hand, Stella laughed. "And miss all of this?"

Despite all the fuss and last-minute panic, this was her and Sean's special day, and Elizabeth couldn't wait to make her vows. She spun to hug her cousin.

"You're right. To quote our Mrs. Mary, 'I wouldn't miss it for the world.'"

MAGGIE SAT in the front row beside Mrs. Mary. Olivia had decorated the open-air chapel beautifully. Garlands of delicate pink rosebuds encircled each post and wove in and out of the white timber trellis at the front.

Standing before the trellis, Frank waited with Sean and Josh for Elizabeth and Stella. Sarah's husband, Mick, was walking Elizabeth down the aisle, her father having died two years ago. Her mother had said she'd try to come, but Elizabeth hadn't been surprised when she didn't. Maggie felt for Liz, but she didn't seem disappointed. Her mother had remarried and now lived in Spain, and she and Elizabeth hadn't seen eye to eye for many years. Was Liz carrying deep-seated hurt that God would cause her to face one day, just like Sean had faced with his father two days ago?

Maggie and Frank had been praying for reconciliation between the pair for so long. Frank had spoken to his brother about Sean and assured him that, since almost dying, his son was a changed man. Stephen had seemed to soften a little. What a blessing to have the barrier between them eradicated.

And then there was Joshua. What a responsible husband and father he'd become. He doted on little Esther, such an adorable baby, and the love he bore for Stella was evident for all to see. God had done amazing work in these two men who'd once been young and reckless, changing them from the inside out and giving them new hearts. Hearts open to love and ready to extend the forgiveness they'd received from the Lord to others.

Maggie would never forget the reconciliation between Joshua and Julian moments before Julian's last breath. God might not have caused his death, but He'd used it for good. It had changed Joshua, and in its turn, Sean.

And now, these two fine young men stood in front of the man she loved the most. How her heart burst with love for this man God had brought into her life. His gaze lifted to hers as if he knew she was thinking about him. When she smiled, he smiled back, and her heart warmed further.

WHEN SEAN TURNED and saw Liz walking towards him, his jaw dropped. Wow. Just wow. Having a do like this was worth it just to see her in her wedding gown. How had he gotten so lucky?

Rows of chairs flanked the makeshift aisle, and guests who cared about them filled those chairs, a hundred of them according to the invitations. But he had eyes only for her. Elizabeth Martin. His bride. His beloved.

As she drew closer, his heart pounded, but when their gazes met and she smiled, it was just him and her.

When Uncle Mick placed her hand in his, Sean squeezed it and grinned. "Hey."

"Hey yourself."

They faced Uncle Frank, who smiled at them before welcoming everyone to the wedding of Sean Robert Goddard and Elizabeth Jean Martin.

"I feel blessed to be presiding over this ceremony. Both Sean and Elizabeth are dear to me, and it's a privilege to be standing here before them—finally. Will you pray with me?"

As Uncle Frank bowed his head, Sean winked at Liz before bowing his own. He sure had God to thank for getting them to this day. He'd never forget how close he'd come to drowning and how grateful he was when Caleb found him. One minute longer, and this day would never have happened.

Uncle Frank's voice rang out clear and loud. "Lord God, we come before You today with thanksgiving in our hearts for bringing these two special people together. Bless their union and give them many happy years together in marriage. I pray this in the name of our Lord and Saviour, Jesus Christ. Amen."

"Amen." Sean raised his head and filled his lungs.

"Stella will now bring us the Bible reading." Uncle Frank nodded to the woman who'd first introduced Liz to him all those years ago when he was bad news. What she'd seen in him, he had no idea. But praise God, she'd seen something and stuck by him.

Stella's rose-coloured dress brushed the ground as she walked. She looked pretty trim after having a baby months ago. He somehow doubted Liz would look so trim after giving birth. But it didn't matter. He'd love her whatever she looked like.

Stella smiled first at them and then at the congregation before opening her Bible and clearing her throat. "Today's reading is a compilation of verses chosen by Sean and Elizabeth. I pray they'll be a blessing to you as well.

"'Place me like a seal over your heart, like a seal on your arm; for love is as strong as death, its jealousy unyielding as the grave. It burns like blazing fire, like a mighty flame. Many waters cannot quench love; rivers cannot sweep it away. If one were to give all the wealth of one's house for love, it would be utterly scorned.

"'Love is patient, love is kind. It does not envy, it does not boast, it is not proud. It does not dishonour others, it is not self-seeking, it is not easily angered, it keeps no record of wrongs. Love does not delight in evil but rejoices with the truth. It always protects, always trusts, always hopes, always perseveres. Love never fails.

"'My command is this: Love each other as I have loved you.'"

Stella lifted her gaze, beaming, then closed her Bible, and took her place at Elizabeth's side.

As Uncle Frank announced a hymn would be next, Sean was still mulling over the verses. Particularly the verses from

CHRISTMAS AT GODDARD DOWNS

the Song of Songs as they spoke of passion, risk, and gain. No doubt his and Liz's marriage would be filled with all three. Nothing boring for them.

He'd need to work at the patience and kind bits. But he wasn't on his own. God was with him, teaching him love, patience, kindness, and all those other fruits he and Liz had been studying together. He had a long way to go, but he was sure grateful that not only Liz but also God were on his side.

The ceremony continued, and then came the time to make their vows. They'd written their own, something he'd found difficult. He was a cowboy, not a writer. But Liz had told him to write from the heart.

Well, he was about to bare his all. Uncle Frank gave him the nod. Sean took Elizabeth's hand, looked deep into her eyes, and cleared his throat. "Liz, I don't deserve you. Everyone knows that. I'm just the scumbag loser who swung by here one day and happened to meet the most gorgeous woman in the world. I don't know what you see in me, but I see the world in you. You're not only beautiful, you're also the kindest, gentlest soul I know. Plus, you have a wicked sense of humour. I love you with every fibre of my being, and with God's help, I promise to love and cherish you and to be faithful to you until death parts us."

He took the ring from Josh, a delicate twist of white gold to match her engagement ring.

Beaming, Liz lifted her hand as he slipped the ring onto her finger.

Then it was her turn. He was expecting hers to be more eloquent than his, but her words came from her heart and almost brought him to tears. "Sean, you're an amazing person.

I know you've battled with self-doubt, but I see so much potential in you. I'm so looking forward to spending the rest of my life with you, and I promise to love and cherish you until we're parted by death. You're the love of my life, and I thank God that He brought us together."

She slipped a matching wedding band onto his finger, but had trouble getting it past his stubby knuckles.

"Sorry." He grimaced.

She chuckled. "It's okay. Once it's on, it'll never come off."

Good point. Not that he'd want to take it off. Ever.

Finally, it slipped past that knuckle, and everyone cheered.

Then Uncle Frank asked, "Sean, will you take Elizabeth to be your wife?"

"You bet!"

Chuckles came from the congregation,

Uncle Frank continued. "Elizabeth, will you take Sean to be your husband?"

Her beam grew. "Absolutely."

"Wonderful! I now pronounce you man and wife! Sean, you may now kiss your bride."

Sean gazed into Liz's eyes before closing the gap between them and taking her in his arms. He brushed her sweet lips with his and drank in the reality that she was now his wife. They were married. For better or worse, for richer or poorer, they were husband and wife.

"I love you, Liz."

His voice, just a whisper, must've been loud enough for her to hear because she replied with those words he'd never tire of hearing, "And I love you, Sean."

The ceremony ended with them walking down the aisle to

the cheers of their family and friends. He stopped and shook hands with his dad, surprised when Dad stepped forward and hugged him. Whoa. They'd figured things out, but since when did Dad hug anyone? That was a bit crazy. But it felt good.

Next, he bent down and hugged his mother. Her cheeks were smeared, and as she reached for him, he felt bad he'd neglected her. He'd visit his parents more often. Who knew how long his mother had left? God did. Sean had no idea, but his near-death experience had taught him how fragile life was and how important it was to tell and show those you loved how much you cared. And to do it often.

Uncle Frank hugged him, as did Maggie. Sean bent down and hugged his grandmother. Once again, only God knew how long she had left. But with her stubbornness, she could outlive them all.

And then came the photos. When Liz had told him how long they might take, he'd balked, but now the time had come, he was okay with it. As long as he was with her, he didn't care how long they took.

The reception was being held on the grassed area outside the homestead. They didn't want anything fancy. He and Liz would have been happy with a barbecue, but Maggie had insisted they do it properly. Janella had come all the way from Darwin to cater for it and brought Jonah and Wade to help.

The spread laid out before them was amazing. So much gourmet food he'd not seen the likes of before. And now he was glad Maggie had insisted. He could get used to this.

After the meal, he took Liz in his arms, and they shared their first dance as husband and wife. Not that he could dance. He had two left feet and no idea how to waltz.

But he could hold Liz and snuggle close.

And that's what they did.

His heart was full. God had blessed him in every way imaginable. What a blessed man he was.

EVERY GOOD AND perfect gift is from above, coming down from the Father of the heavenly lights, who does not change like shifting shadows (James 1:17).

A NOTE FROM THE AUTHOR

I hope you enjoyed this final book in *The Sunburned Land Series*. I have to admit that I shed a tear or two as I said goodbye to Frank and Maggie and their families. Over the period of the past year or so they've become so close to me that I feel I know them like I know my own family.

My prayer is that their daily reliance on God will encourage you in your own walk with the Lord. We were never promised a life without troubles, but God did promise that He'd be us through every trial we face, and that 'those who hope in the Lord will renew their strength. They will soar on wings like eagles; they will run and not grow weary, they will walk and not be faint.'

May God richly bless you today and always.

So, what comes next? Well, I have many books and series you can choose from, however, you might be interested to know that there's a Sunburned Land prequel series, called *'Beneath the Southern Cross'*. It's set in the late 1800's and goes into the 1900's, and tells the story of the Goddard family and how they established Goddard Downs, and yes, Mrs. Mary and young Frank will make an appearance in Book 4 (yet to be written!). At the time of writing, there are two books in the series: "Love's Unwavering Hope" and "Love's Rebellious Spirit". Book three, "Love's Distant Dream" is coming soon! The first two paperback books can be purchased from my store .

I also have another 'mature-age' series you might like: *A*

Time for Everything Series. You can get discounted ebook and paperback bundles from my store.

I've included part of the first chapter of both of these series in the following pages.

Lastly, I'd be thrilled if you could spend a few moments and leave a review. Reviews truly make a difference and help other readers decide if they want to read a book or not. Thank you in advance!

Until next time, take care and God bless.

Juliette

LOVE'S UNWAVERING HOPE (PREVIEW)

CHAPTER 1

*L*ove's Unwavering Hope - Book 1 in the "Beneath the Southern Cross - Dawn of the Sunburned Land Series"

Prologue

Gippsland, Victoria, 1882

The Cobb and Co coach jostled its passengers, every bump in the road resonating through its timeworn frame. The wheels' creaks and groans echoed the pulsating ache in seventeen-year-old Eliza Reynolds's temples. For three days, she and her twelve-year-old brother, Thomas, had been travelling, first by carriage, then by train, and now by coach, after their father sent word that their home in Gippsland was ready.

In Melbourne these past four months, she and Thomas had felt far from welcome with distant relatives in an already crowded house. Then the promise of a better life in Australia had seemed but a distant dream.

The unimaginable marred their voyage on the *SS Sovereign*

Star. Fever cruelly claimed their mother. The memory of her body, veiled by the dark cloak of the sea, was still raw. Their father had been a broken man, and their collective grief felt insurmountable. But their parents' shared dream—a dream whispered in the corners of their tiny London flat—had propelled Father to venture into Australia's wild terrain, seeking out the land they dreamed of.

Now, Gippsland's savage beauty unfurled outside the coach window, its sprawling pastures dotted with livestock and shadowed by towering eucalyptus trees. The sun-drenched terrain, while beautiful, also stood as a stark reminder of how far they were from their London home.

Thomas leaned against her. "How much longer, Eliza?"

Her lips curved as she ruffled his wavy brown hair. "I believe Baker's Run is close."

He tipped his head upwards. "Do you think Father will be there to meet us?"

"He knows our journey's schedule. He should be." She couldn't share her doubts. Her brother already suffered too much. But those doubts clenched her jaw. Had living in this new country changed Father, or was he still the moody and unpredictable man he'd always been? *God, please, let him have changed.*

Thomas, his voice tinged with the innocence of youth and shadows of past sorrows, whispered, "What's our new life going to be like?"

Heart softening, she replied, "It's going to be wonderful."

"I do hope so." He jiggled in his seat, displaying his first eagerness in months. "Maybe Father got the ponies Mother promised us."

She hesitated, thinking of their father's inconsistent nature. "Time will reveal all, dear brother." Straightening, she pointed to a distant collection of buildings. "I do believe that's Baker's Run."

I hope you enjoyed the beginning of "Love's Unwavering Hope". To continue reading, go to: www.julietteduncanbookstore.com/collections/beneath-the-southern-cross-the-dawn-of-a-sunburned-land-series

A TIME TO TREASURE
(PREVIEW)

CHAPTER 1

*S*ydney, Australia

Wendy Miller rigidly held her tears in check when her eldest daughter, Natalie, slipped on her beautiful wedding gown. The strapless A-line style suited Natalie's slim figure perfectly, but the prospect of her daughter walking down the aisle without her father brought a massive lump to Wendy's throat.

Wendy's husband, Greg, had suffered a fatal heart attack four years earlier, and although the pain she felt whenever she thought of him had lessened to a dull ache, it was moments like these that brought it rushing back.

"How does it look, Mum?" Natalie stood in front of the full-length mirror, peering over her shoulder at the back of the gown, while Roxanne, the gown's creator, adjusted the straps.

"It's perfect, sweetheart. You're going to be a gorgeous bride."

Relief filled Natalie's face. "Thank you."

"Your father would have been so proud to walk you down the aisle in this," Wendy added in a wistful tone.

"Mum! You need to stop saying that. It's hard enough as it is."

Wendy bit her lip. Natalie was right. They were both struggling, and Natalie didn't need constant reminders that her father wouldn't be there on her special day when it no doubt was on her mind anyway. Wendy reached out and rubbed Natalie's arm. "I know, sweetheart, I'm sorry."

Natalie stood completely still while Roxanne inspected the gown, making the odd adjustment here and there. Dressed in an oversized multi-coloured loose-fitting shirt, purple tights and yellow sneakers, the young woman didn't look like one of Sydney's top fashion designers, but Roxanne Alexander was a multi-award winner eagerly sought after by the well-to-do, and they'd been fortunate to engage her services. "I won't do the final adjustments until the week before the wedding, but other than that, I think it's done," Roxanne said as she straightened.

Natalie beamed. "I love it so much. Thank you. Now all I have to do is eat salad for the next three months."

Roxanne laughed. "I wouldn't worry about that. A few extra pounds won't matter."

"Great! I wasn't looking forward to starving myself."

Wendy chuckled. Her daughter was as thin as a rake, even though she had a voracious appetite. "I don't think there's any chance of that. Come on, get dressed and I'll buy you lunch."

While Roxanne helped Natalie out of the gown, Wendy inspected the bridesmaids' dresses, which Roxanne also had designed. Paige, Wendy's youngest daughter, had been less than co-operative and showed little interest in her sister's wedding, turning up only once for a fitting. Wendy sometimes wondered if she'd even turn up for the wedding. She sighed heavily. It wasn't helpful comparing her children, but Natalie and Paige were so different. And then there was Simon…

"See you next time." Roxanne waved as Wendy and Natalie headed for the door.

"We'll look forward to it." Wendy smiled and then followed Natalie to the lift. While they waited, Wendy slipped her arm around Natalie's waist. "I'm sorry I get teary so often. It's… well, you know?"

"It's okay Mum. I understand. I wish Dad was here, too."

"I know you do, sweetheart."

The lift arrived and the doors opened. Stepping inside, they rode down the four levels, emerging into the foyer of the high-end building in downtown Sydney.

"Where would you like to go?" Wendy asked.

Natalie shrugged. "I don't mind, your choice."

"Okay. I know just the place." Wendy linked her arm through Natalie's and together they headed out into the bustling city. Taxis honked, moving like snails through the congested streets. Shoppers strolled along the footpath, chatting, pausing to look in shop windows, oblivious of the office workers weaving around them, hurrying to grab a quick midday meal before returning to their respective offices for the afternoon.

The aroma of freshly baked pizza wafted from an Italian restaurant, mingling with the scent of hot dogs piled high on a vendor's cart at the corner of Edward and King. "I wouldn't mind pizza," Natalie remarked, looking longingly over her shoulder while they waited for the lights to change.

"That's not really what I had in mind," Wendy said.

"What's wrong with pizza?"

Wendy laughed. "Nothing. Nothing at all. You know how much I love Italian food. I was just thinking of your waistline and your wedding dress." Wendy paused and then leaned in close to her daughter. "To be quite honest, I'm mostly worried about the mother-of-the-bride dress!"

The lights changed and Natalie giggled as they joined the crush of pedestrians crossing to the other side. They walked on in comfortable silence, Natalie seemingly content to follow Wendy, and several minutes later, they arrived at one of Wendy's favourite restaurants. One she and Greg had dined at often. Maybe it wasn't the wisest choice, but she couldn't think of a nicer place to lunch with her daughter.

When the maître d' greeted them, Wendy asked for an outdoor table.

"Of course, Mrs. Miller, follow me," the smartly dressed young woman replied.

Natalie raised a brow at her mother and walked beside her to the table on the balcony that the maître d' chose for them. After the young woman settled them in and promised to send a waiter to take their orders, Natalie leaned forward. "We didn't have to come here, Mum. It'll cost a fortune!"

"It's okay, darling. I wanted to spoil you," Wendy replied, trying hard to keep her voice steady. The restaurant had one of the best views of the harbour and the Opera House, and on this perfect spring day, the water glistening in the sunshine was just glorious. Just like the days when she and Greg came here…

"You don't need to," Natalie replied. She grew silent for a few seconds, her face paling. Grabbing Wendy's arm, she asked, "Are you okay, Mum?"

Wendy frowned. "Of course I am. What makes you think I'm not?"

"You look tired, that's all. And bringing me here…" Natalie's voice trailed away, but Wendy could see fear in her daughter's eyes.

"You wonder if I'm sick?"

"Yes."

Wendy squeezed Natalie's hand. "I'm fine. Nothing to worry about. Honestly."

"Are you sure?" Natalie asked, frowning.

"Positive!"

A male waiter approached and stopped beside the table. The two women grabbed their menus and quickly perused them.

"Are you ready to order, ladies, or shall I come back?" the well-groomed, dark-haired young man asked politely.

"Could you give us a few minutes, please?" Wendy removed her designer sunglasses and smiled at him.

"Of course." He poured two glasses of water from the jug on the table and stepped aside.

"There's no pizza on the menu," Natalie whispered loudly.

Wendy laughed. "You don't need pizza, Natalie."

"I know." Natalie chuckled. "Shall we share the paella instead?"

Wendy set her menu on the table and smiled lovingly at her daughter. "Good choice." She waved the waiter over and placed the order. After he left, she slipped her sunglasses back on, sipped her water, and studied her daughter. What would she do without Natalie? Soon, her eldest daughter would be married and have less time to spend with her mother. The thought saddened Wendy, but she knew she had to deal with it. She couldn't, but more importantly, wouldn't, impose on Natalie and Adam. The first year of marriage was such a special time. Even now, after all the years that had passed, memories of her first year with Greg filled her with such warmth. They'd had a wonderful marriage. But it was no good constantly reminiscing. Although he'd be waiting for her in the life to come, he was gone from this earth, and she had to accept that fact and try to build a new life on her own.

"Have you spoken to Simon lately?" Natalie asked.

Wendy blinked and returned her attention to Natalie. "Not for a few weeks. He's replied to a few texts, but I think he's super busy with work. Did you know he got a promotion?"

Natalie frowned again. "No. He's always busy when I call. Makes me think he doesn't want to talk to me anymore."

"You know your brother. When he doesn't want to talk, he doesn't want to talk. But when he chooses to, you can't stop him."

"Yes, but surely he can find time to talk to *you* at least once a week. You're his mother, after all."

"I've come to the conclusion that we have to give him space," Wendy replied as positively as she could, because, the truth was, she also wondered why Simon found it so hard to keep in touch, but she *was* his mother, and she wouldn't speak ill of him with his sister.

Natalie crossed her arms. "If he keeps this up much longer, I'm going to drive to his house and make him talk. I mean it!"

"Don't be like that, sweetheart. He doesn't like it when we pressure him, you know that."

"I don't understand him! You'd think with Dad gone, he'd be more attentive of you."

"I can look after myself. But I agree, it'd be lovely to see more of him."

The waiter approached and set the paella on the table between them. "Would you like me to serve?" he asked.

Wendy flashed an appreciative smile. "We'll be fine, thanks. It smells wonderful."

The waiter nodded, refilled their glasses, and wished them *bon appétit* before leaving them to their meal.

"Pass your plate, Mum," Natalie said, holding her hand out.

Wendy complied and Natalie heaped several spoons of the colourful dish onto the middle of the plate. Wendy held her hand up. "That's plenty, darling. Thank you."

"Are you sure? There's a lot here."

"Yes, that's fine."

Natalie filled her plate and then quickly scooped a huge spoonful into her mouth, releasing a pleasurable sigh. Wendy was glad the conversation about Simon had been dropped. His lack of communication did worry her, and she often wondered if something was wrong, but didn't want Natalie concerned about him with her wedding fast approaching. Wendy decided to call him again when she got home.

After making quick work of the paella, Natalie leaned back in her chair and placed her hands across her stomach. "So, what have you decided about the trip?"

Wendy sipped her iced tea and released a long sigh. Greg's grandmother, who lived just south of London, was turning ninety, and Wendy had booked a trip to the U.K. to attend the celebration. She'd also invited her friend, Robyn, to accompany her, but now Robyn couldn't go because her mother had taken ill, and Wendy was considering cancelling. She set her glass on the table and toyed with her fork. "I don't think I'll go."

"Oh Mum, I think you should. Since Dad's death, you've hardly taken a holiday—I think it'll do you good."

"But on my own?"

Natalie chuckled. "You never know, you might meet a handsome gentleman who'll sweep you off your feet!"

"Natalie!"

"Sorry..." A playful grin had spread across Natalie's face. She leaned forward, crossing her arms on the table. "Seriously, I think you should go. You've travelled a lot, you'll be fine. You need to go, Mum."

Wendy sighed heavily. "I'll give it some more thought. If I stay home, I can help more with the wedding preparations."

"You've already done more than enough. It's all in hand," Natalie replied with just a hint of exasperation in her voice.

"I know. But it seems strange to think of travelling to the other side of the world without your dad. It won't be the same."

Natalie squeezed her mother's hand. "I know. But go. Do it for Dad."

Wendy grimaced and swallowed the lump in her throat. "I'll think about it, but right now, I think I'd like coffee. Would you like one?"

"That would be lovely. Thank you."

Wendy beckoned the waiter over and ordered two cups.

"And can I tempt you with the dessert menu?" He quirked a brow as he held out two.

Wendy smiled politely. "Thank you, but no. Coffee will be fine."

Natalie leaned forward again after the waiter left, her face filled with disappointment. "I was going to order something," she said in a sulky tone.

Wendy chuckled, shaking her head. "You do take after your father with your sweet tooth."

"I can't help it," Natalie replied defensively, but then she laughed.

"I guess not. But even though Roxanne said it didn't matter, you should still watch what you're eating." Wendy quickly bit her lip. She shouldn't have said that. Natalie was a grown woman and could make her own decisions about what to eat and what to avoid. Thank goodness Natalie had an understanding nature. Paige would never have let her get away with saying anything like that. "I'm sorry darling. Have whatever you want." Wendy smiled and beckoned the waiter again.

To continue reading A Time to Treasure, go to: www.julietteduncanbookstore.com/products/a-time-for-everything-series-box-set-books-1-4-a-christian-romance-paperback-edition

OTHER BOOKS BY JULIETTE DUNCAN

Find all of Juliette Duncan's books on her websites:

www.julietteduncan.com/library

www.julietteduncanbookstore.com

Beneath the Southern Cross: The Dawn of a Sunburned Land Series

Love's Unwavering Hope

Love's Rebellious Spirit

Love's Distant Dream

Love's Precious Moments

Love's Faithful Journey (Coming 2026)

A Sunburned Land Series

Slow Road to Love

Slow Path to Peace

Slow Ride Home

Slow Dance at Dusk

Slow Trek to Triumph

Christmas at Goddard Downs

True Love Series

Tender Love

Tested Love

Tormented Love

Triumphant Love

Transformed by Love Christian Romance Series

Because We Loved

Because We Forgave

Because We Dreamed

Because We Believed

Because We Cared

Billionaires with Heart Series

Her Kind-Hearted Billionaire

Her Generous Billionaire

Her Disgraced Billionaire

Her Compassionate Billionaire

The Potter's House Books...

The Homecoming

Unchained

Blessings of Love

The Hope We Share

The Love Abounds

Love's Healing Touch

Melody of Love

Whispers of Hope

Promise of Peace

Heroes Of Eastbrooke Christian Romance Suspense Series

Safe in His Arms

Under His Watch

Within His Sight

Freed by His Love

ABOUT THE AUTHOR

Juliette Duncan is passionate about writing true to life Christian romances that will touch her readers' hearts and make a difference in their lives. Drawing on her own often challenging real-life experiences, Juliette writes deeply emotional stories that highlight God's amazing love and faithfulness, for which she's eternally grateful. Juliette lives on the beautiful Sunshine Coast of Queensland, Australia, and she and her husband have five adult children and eleven grandchildren. When not writing, Juliette and her husband love exploring the great outdoors.

Connect with Juliette:

Email: author@julietteduncan.com

Website: www.julietteduncan.com

Juliette's bookstore: www.julietteduncanbookstore.com

Facebook: www.facebook.com/JulietteDuncanAuthor

BookBub: www.bookbub.com/authors/juliette-duncan

www.ingramcontent.com/pod-product-compliance
Lightning Source LLC
Chambersburg PA
CBHW070611120726
47909CB00004B/1169

* 9 7 8 0 6 4 8 9 4 2 8 7 0 *